Pride & Premiership

Michelle Gayle's career has spanned TV, theatre, film and music. She was first known for her TV appearances, which began in the 1980s with children's drama *Grange Hill*, followed by *EastEnders*, before she moved over to a glittering pop career that saw her achieve six top twenty hits and sell a million records, most successfully her 1994 single "Sweetness". Michelle has since appeared on TV shows such as *Reborn in the USA*, *Doctors*, *Holby City*, *Family Affairs* and *The Games*, and she starred opposite Ed Stoppard in the 2006 film *Joy Division*. In recent years Michelle has presented on *Loose Women* and also taken part in reality TV shows *Come Dine with Me* and *Dancing on Wheels*. Michelle now lives with her partner and son in west London; this is her first novel.

This book is also available as an eBook
or mobile-phone download. To find out more,
visit **www.gospoken.com** and search for
Pride and Premiership.

Pride & Premiership

MICHELLE GAYLE

WALKER
BOOKS

This is a work of fiction. Names, characters, places and incidents
are either the product of the author's imagination or, if real, are used
fictitiously. All statements, activities, stunts, descriptions, information
and material of any other kind contained herein are included for
entertainment purposes only and should not be relied on for
accuracy or replicated, as they may result in injury.

First published 2011 by Walker Books Ltd
87 Vauxhall Walk, London SE11 5HJ

2 4 6 8 10 9 7 5 3 1

Text © 2011 Michelle Gayle
Cover design by Walker Books Ltd
Shoes provided by Miss Selfridge (**www.missselfridge.com**)

The right of Michelle Gayle to be identified as author of this
work has been asserted by her in accordance with the
Copyright, Designs and Patents Act 1988

This book has been typeset in Fairfield

Printed and bound in Great Britain by Clays Ltd, St Ives plc

British Library Cataloguing in Publication Data:
a catalogue record for this book is available from the British Library

ISBN 978-1-4063-3088-5

www.walker.co.uk

www.undercoverreads.com

For Isaiah and Tony

Quick Response bar codes are the ultimate tool for accessing extra content. First, go to **http://gettag.mobi** on your phone to download the Microsoft Tag Reader application. Then use the app to scan the bar codes throughout this book.

Scan the code below to watch a video of Michelle introducing *Pride & Premiership*:

Get the free mobile app at http://gettag.mobi

This is the diary of Remy Louise Bennet.
Read it (Mum) and I'll never record
Corrie or EastEnders for you again!

Remy + Leonardo DiCaprio 4ever!

Shia La"Buff"
– Phwoar!!

Team Edward ☺

scan the code to watch a video
of Michelle Gayle reading from this book:

Sunday 22 June – 2.30 a.m.

Oh–hhh M–mmm G–gggg. I've just snogged a Premier-ship footballer! His name's Robbie Wilkins and he plays for Netherfield Park Rangers. OK, it's not a massive club like Man United, or Chelsea, which Gary (the one Malibu got off with) happens to play for. But Robbie's still a good catch. Malibu says that players at smaller clubs get about £20,000 a week. TWENTY GRAND!! That's more than I'll make in a year manicuring and waxing people at Kara's.

Robbie is twenty-one and blonde, with highlights – eugh! (Highlights will have to go.) But apart from his hair (and slightly big nose), he's buff beyond belief.

He's proper charming, too. He told me I look like a young Julia Roberts. ☺

Although, to be honest, I don't think he'd have noticed

me if it hadn't been for Malibu's plan. That girl is so clued up. She went to the Lounge four times just to do her research and has seen six different Premiership players there! Apparently they usually sit in the VIP area in the back of the club and they're always surrounded by girls who act like lap dancers in front of them, or reach over to pass them their phone number.

"If they get lucky, some girls even leave with a player or two," said Malibu. "But we're not aiming for that."

"Huh?" I went, confused.

"No," she said firmly. "The same players come back the next week, blank the girls who were all over them last time and move on to a fresh set. We're real WAG material, Remy. Not bloody wannabes."

Yeah, right, I thought. I mean, Malibu is WAG material all day long – blonde, skinny, big boobs (lucky cow) – but ME? I didn't think I'd stand a chance, but my genius sister had it all worked out.

Her carefully calculated strategy was for us to separate ourselves from the WAG wannabes as soon as we got there.

"They're so–oo easy," she said, "and boys, especially footballers, are all about the chase." (See what I mean about being clued up?)

When we arrived there was a massive line of people waiting to get in, and when we finally got up to the door, the bouncer double-, triple-checked my fake ID. I thought he was going to turn me away, so I threw him a massive smile and made my eyes say, "Purle–eeeease."

"Go on then," he said.

Sucka! ☺

The Lounge is like nowhere I've ever been before. Everything about it says: money.

It also happened to be full of good-looking girls aiming to pull themselves a footballer. And with me in my white jeans and Primarni sparkly top, and Malibu in her denim jumpsuit, we looked like we were going skiing compared with those WAG wannabes. They were half bloody naked!

The boys there weren't exactly shy either. I got my first chat-up line within ten minutes: "Get your coat – we're going home," he said.

"We're not interested!" Malibu snapped before I could say a word.

The WAG wannabes weren't interested either. They were turning boys away big time, waiting for the real deal – and then … Robbie and Gary stepped through the door. I knew they were footballers straight away. I'd like to say it was because I'd done my research (like Malibu) or because they were dressed immaculately (which they were) and walked with a swagger (which they did). But, to be honest, the only reason I knew they were footballers was because those WAG wannabes swarmed round them like bees to a jar of honey.

Robbie and Gary fought their way through the heaving breasts and plonked themselves down in the VIP area. Then Malibu looked at me, gave me a wink, and we strutted straight past them without (and this was important) even glancing their way, and hit the dance floor. This worked out perfectly for me because Malibu may be the blonde, prettier and skinnier one, with those boobs, of course (which just isn't fair), but she can't dance to save her life! When "Crazy in Love" started, she looked like she was having a fit, while I did the dance that Beyoncé does in the video – "Uh-oh, uh-oh, uh-oh…" And that's when Robbie tapped my shoulder and asked me to go outside with him for some "fresh air".

We talked about the usual at first – what's your name, age, etc. And when I told him it was my half-birthday tomorrow, he said it was a cool thing to celebrate.

"Thanks," I replied.

"Pleasure," he said, then he threw me a look that made my stomach do a double somersault.

I knew what was coming next and couldn't wait – but also remembered what Malibu had said about how if a girl holds out, a footballer will want her more because they love to win. So (gutted) I told him I was only up for kissing.

"That's new." He smiled. And then we got STUCK IN!

His kisses were a bit sloppy, to be honest, but I put that down to him having had a few drinks. Anyway, who cares? When our lips unlocked, we exchanged numbers and he said he was dying to see me again. Just like Malibu predicted.

She did a right number on Gary, too. When Robbie walked me back inside, we couldn't find them for ages.

So I decided to check whether she was in the loo and spotted her and Gary propped up against the wall beside the fire exit – snogging!!

"Your sister," Gary said when he realized I was gawping at them, "is the most stunning girl I've ever met." ☺

Malibu's proper. She says it's a big sister's job to educate. And she's put all her years of reading every WAG interview ever to good use by making the WAG Charter. It's a five-point plan that Malibu reckons will get us a footballer quicker than we can say Frank Lampard. And it seems to be working. Yay!

I'm going to write it down so that in weak moments I can look at it and think of the big picture, because I'd love to marry Robbie. So I can jack in my job – and shop FOR THE REST OF MY LIFE!!

THE WAG CHARTER

1. AT FIRST, PRETEND YOU DON'T KNOW HE'S A FOOTBALLER.

2. STICK TO KISSING ON THE FIRST DATE.

3. DON'T LET HIM SEE YOU DRUNK, OR HE WON'T TRUST YOU WHEN HE'S AWAY ON A PRE-SEASON TOUR.

4. WAIT EIGHT WEEKS TO HIT FOURTH BASE. (FOOTBALLERS MARRY "GOOD" GIRLS THEY CAN TAKE HOME TO THEIR MUMS.)

5. NEVER DISPUTE A THING HIS MUM SAYS. (THEY WORSHIP THEIR MUMS.)

2.42 a.m.

PS He's calling at 11 a.m. How will I survive till then?!

2.43 a.m.

PPS I'll only shop half of the time because I'm still going to open a beauty salon that'll blow Kara's out of the water. And I'll pay proper wages that allow my beauticians to buy their own houses, so they won't have to live with their parents, like we do.

2.49 a.m.

PPPS Wondering whether I should take his surname or combine mine with his – Remy Wilkins (hmm). Remy Bennet Wilkins (nah). Remy Wilkins Bennet (has a certain ring to it).

2.55 a.m.

PPPPS Just want to big Malibu up for taking me to the Lounge. It was the best half-birthday present ever! ☺

Eek! Getting this diary from the girls at Kara's is up there too. (Even though my lip curled like it was dog muck when they gave it to me – how was I supposed to know I'd have so much to write about?!)

3.00 a.m.

PPPPPS Eight hours to go!

10.59 a.m.!!!

Phone: Clutched in hand.
    Eyes: Fixed on phone.
    Brain: Counting down! Ten, nine, eight…

11.15 a.m.

No Robbie.

11.25 a.m.

I've been checking my phone like a nutcase. Is it on silent? Have I run out of credit? (Which is stupid because I can still receive calls if I'm out of credit!) Did I accidentally pick up someone else's mobile?

    Answer: No, no and triple no.

11.28 a.m.

Maybe he's asleep. Or… Maybe *I* should phone *him*? But if he didn't mean to call, I'll look like a right idiot! Definitely won't phone first. I have some self-respect.

11.33 a.m.

If I hide my number, call to check whether he's awake, then put the phone down if he answers, will that make me a bunny boiler?

I'll ask Malibu.

11.40 a.m.

I hate Malibu. She said not to call him and – now it's past the thirty-minute deadline – not to answer his call either. So that he can learn to respect me. First of all, the thirty-minute deadline is *her* stupid rule. Second of all, I reckon she was harping on about respect because she's all right ... Gary (Chelsea player) has been texting her ballistically all night. Third of all, she had the nerve to twist the situation by suggesting Robbie probably has a girlfriend and can't phone because he's with her right now. And the only reason I'm not crying is because Mum and Dad called me into the kitchen to give me a half-birthday prezzie: a brand-new pink iPod with a matching base station. Yay! And to top it off, Mum just popped into my room, said she forgot to give me one last thing, then handed over a card from my godfather, Alan, with £100 in it! He's the best. Even though he's lived in Australia since I was ten, he always remembers I celebrate half-birthdays because my real one's so close to Christmas.

Still no Robbie. I'll answer his call, but like an ice queen. "Oh… Robbie who?"

Malibu has apologized. She says I should get myself a fail-safe, which is someone that loves you so much, you can always get back with him if things go wrong with someone else. I asked her why you wouldn't just stick with the fail-safe and she said because they're boring. Then I checked if she had one and she said yes, Roger Miller. (Who's nice but majorly boring.)

"Roger Miller?" I said, surprised.

"Yeah. What's wrong with him?"

"Nothing," I mumbled, but inside I was thinking, *Roger Miller's no Lance Wilson*.

Lance is most definitely the best-looking boyfriend Malibu's ever had. Their relationship was sort of like Carrie and Big's in *Sex and the City* but without the happy ending. (Basically she dumped him because he wouldn't take the relationship to the next level and get engaged.) And now she rips into anyone who says anything good about him.

Anyway, she said no matter how well things go with Gary (Chelsea player), she doesn't trust him as far as she can throw him, and will always keep Roger as her back-up plan.

Now we're going to watch Leonardo DiCaprio in *Romeo and Juliet* for the thousandth time. Malibu knows that Leo always cheers me up. Maybe she's not too bad after all.

Wherefore art thou, Robbie?

10.00 P.M.

He called!

"Happy half-birthday, princess," he whispered.

"You remembered," swooned I.

He had to whisper because he's caught a bad throat infection. Said he couldn't even speak this morning, and that's why he didn't phone. Phew! He wants to take me out on Wednesday. I asked where, but he said he had bad reception, then the line went dead. Got his voicemail when I called back.

10.01 P.M.

Voicemail.

10.02 P.M.

Voicemail.

10.10 P.M.

Voicemail x 12.

Dear God, please don't let Malibu be right about him having a girlfriend!

Over breakfast this morning Malibu bragged that Gary had texted to say she's beautiful. So I bragged that Robbie had called.

"Why did he phone so late?" she asked.

"Because he was sick… With a throat infection."

"Do you believe him?"

I had my doubts, especially when his call ended so suddenly and all I got was his voicemail for the rest of the night – but why tell her that and make him look bad next to Gary Goldenballs?

"Yeah," I said, "he could just about whisper when he spoke to me."

And then she tutted and told me I was so–ooo naïve, as if I was a little kid.

When we got to work, the first thing Malibu did was announce that we'd pulled some footballers. And everyone went, "Woo-oo!"

"Were they fit?" Natasha asked. Which was a bit of a trick question because according to Natasha, not even Brad Pitt is fit.

"My one looks like Will Smith," Malibu said.

Yeah right, I thought.

Then before I could get a word in she told them, "Unfortunately, though, Remy ended up with a tosser." She claimed that Robbie called twelve hours later than he was supposed to. (What a liar! It was ten hours, fifty-six minutes!) "And get this: he was whispering because of a 'throat infection' – purlease," she sneered.

While I stood there cringing, they all debated whether Robbie was lying and does in fact have a girlfriend.

Verdict: Blatantly.

"Told ya he's a lyin', cheatin' toerag!" Malibu shouted, doing her Pat Butcher impression.

I went bright red and fled to the kitchen area.

How humiliating. She should be done for sadism. They should lock her up and bury the bloody key.

When she came to apologize, I pretended I had something in my eye. But she knew I'd been crying. She said she didn't mean to be a cow, she just wanted me to understand that all men are dogs. "But," she added, "a lying, cheating footballer is better than a lying, cheating bin man."

8 P.M.

Can't find the half-birthday card I got from my godfather, which sucks because he wrote his new mobile number in it. OK, I probably wouldn't phone him – Australia kills credit and all that – but I was thinking about surprising him with a thank-you text instead of the usual email. Hmm… Took the money out of it, then I'm sure I put it on the bedside table beside my iPod…

That nosy knickers Nicole Walker just phoned. Haven't hooked up with her since we left school but she still rings every now and then – when she wants to find something out. Nobody loves gossip as much as Nicole.

"A little birdie tells me you've pulled a footballer," she said.

"Might have," I answered with a smirk.

"And apparently he's a right—"

"Nic," I interrupted before she could finish, "I'm in the middle of looking for something. Can I call you back?"

"Oh. All right then."

Bloody hell, news spreads like wildfire in west London.

Now, where's my half-birthday card?

Asked Mum where Godfather Alan's card was, and she said how the hell would she know.

But I bet she moved it when she tidied my room. She's such a cleaning freak! Grr.

Malibu's gone to see Boring Roger. She said that holding out with Gary means she has to get it somewhere.

Before she left, she handed me a box of four Krispy Kreme doughnuts and said, "Forgiven?"

I told her she was.

I love Krispy Kremes, but I'd be proper lardy for my Wednesday night date if I ate all four of them. And the words "fat" and "WAG" just don't go together. FACT. (Posh – boobs on a stick; Alex Curran – skinny; Colleen, my fave, the biggest and a size 10/12 like me, but at least she's blonde.) So basically I can't afford to push it. Gave two to Dad, one to Mum and ate the original glazed one. Still, it's the thought that counts. Malibu's definitely back in my good books.

11.35 P.M.

I was in bed wondering if Robbie really was a lying, cheating scumbag when my phone bleeped and it was a text from him! This coincidence was a sign, proving that he does NOT have a girlfriend.

He wrote: *Gagging 2 c u on Wednesday princess x*

I wrote back: *Can't wait 2 c u 2 gorgeous* ☺

11.45 P.M.

Can't sleep. Mum and Dad are arguing in that hiss they think we can't hear. It works up to a point, but every now and then they lose control and the odd word or phrase pops out.

Dad: "IT'S something, something, something, TO GO BEHIND MY BACK!"

Mum: "Something, something WORRY something, something, something, THOUSANDS OF MILES AWAY."

Dad: "YOU'RE ONE TO something PREACH!"

Now Mum's crying.

Please don't break up again. At least not until I've bought a house and moved out.

Tuesday 24 June – 8.30 a.m.

Can't believe I ate that Krispy Kreme last night. Especially when I'm going out with Robbie tomorrow. And especially when I know that Fat Girl + Footballer = Impossibility. Doh! This is my chance to shop till I drop, get my own magazine column (like Alex) or my own TV programme (like Coleen) and I'm blowing it. Big time. So, no more thigh-bulging, bum-spreading doughnuts. Today is detox day, which means I will stick strictly to water, lettuce leaves and one apple.

(To the tune of "Rehab") *Try to make me eat a Krispy and I'll say, 'No, no, no.'* "

6.25 p.m.

Malibu's a dark horse. Turns out she's going out with Gary Goldenballs tonight. And I only heard about it at work, when Blow-dry Sarah told me. (We'd gone on a coffee run.)

"Oi!" I hissed to Malibu when I got back. "When did Blow-dry become your news feed?"

Allegedly the date was arranged at the last minute and Blow-dry only knew about it because she was covering Malibu's 5 p.m. pedicure so that Malibu could leave work early. Blow-dry is Malibu's lackey. But still, I'm her sister – she's supposed to tell me first!

Anyhoo. Looked for date outfits in my lunch break. And because of my generous godfather, I could actually afford to go into Warehouse and Oasis. ☺ Shopping helped take my mind off how starving I was too. How the hell do models live on lettuce leaves? They taste like crap (no matter how much salt you put on them).

I bought an LBD, a flowery maxi dress and some killer heels. And now I'm going to eat an apple. Yesss!

7 P.M.

OMG! Malibu's wearing high-waisted hot pants with a black vest and black-patent wedges for her date with Goldenballs. Before she left work Natasha topped up her spray tan, so she looks double, triple hot. She put on a French accent and said to me, "Monsieur Gary Johnson weell find me irreeseestible."

"Remember you've got to hold out," I reminded her.

"Of course. It's my bloody rule," she replied.

She's meeting him at the top of our road because she doesn't want Mum and Dad sticking their noses in.

I asked her why. Mum would love to know she's finally pulled a footballer.

"Yeah, but she'll probably make it really obvious that it's her dream come true and scare him off. He's not in the bag yet… Plus Dad will just give him the eyes," she added, imitating the look Dad gives to boys when we first bring them home. The one that says, "Mess with my girl and I'll knock you into next week!" And we giggled.

"Good point," I told her.

When she was leaving, Dad said, "You can't go out like that!"

And Mum shouted at him, "Just bloody leave her alone," because she's still upset with Dad after their (secret) argument last night.

7.45 P.M.

Googled Robbie and zoomed in on a picture of him in his football kit. He has thighs like a Greek god! His birthday's on 3 November, which makes him a Scorpio – just like Leonardo DiCaprio. And there's no mention of a girlfriend. Yesss! Move over Leonardo, there's a new Scorpio in town.

7.51 P.M.

I'm depressed. Went on Robbie's Facebook page and it's full of blonde, skinny "friends" with pneumatic bazookas. Need to lose weight, pronto! ☹

<u>Wednesday 25 June – 2.30 a.m.</u>

Malibu woke me up to boast about eating in a posh restaurant called Nobu.

She said Gary has a Bentley convertible and it's like riding around on a £120,000 sofa. One hundred and twenty grand!! That could buy me a flat!

"What car does Robbie drive?" she asked.

I shrugged, then moaned, "I was sleeping, you know."

Now feel guilty about cutting her off in her prime, but think I'm still hurt that Blow-dry Sarah knew she was going out with Gary before me. ☹

Plus I'm bloody starving!! ☹

And I need beauty sleep for my big date tomorrow. (Can't believe I'm going out with an actual Premiership footballer!) ☺

Now I feel like this: ☺ ☹ ☺ ☹ ☺

scan the code for extra content

Date Night!!!! – 8.10 a.m.

Robbie just texted: *Will pick you up at 6 princess. Just tell me where.* x

So I gave him the salon address. (Malibu's right – don't need Mum or Dad getting involved this early.)

It's so–oo exciting!

8.20 a.m.

Shall I wear the new LBD or the maxi dress? Hmm... I'll phone Kellie and see what she thinks.

8.22 a.m.

Kellie said she can't tell without seeing them both. She's

the crappiest best friend ever. I'll phone my BMF – James is a fashion guru, he'll know.

Just remembered, James isn't my best male friend any more – after our little disagreement about me "borrowing" his GHDs. ☹ I managed to end the call a microsecond before his phone rang. Phew!

As Robbie's picking me up from work, I'll take both dresses in with me and see what the girls think.

Used the lunch break to bring the maxi dress back home because all the girls agreed that the LBD was better. Well, actually, all except that feminazi Kara. She thought I should wear the maxi dress because it left more to the imagination, and when I chose the LBD she went into one and said it was too short.

Why on earth does she think it's called a LITTLE black dress?!

Whatever.

Now Malibu has just called and wound me up even more. "Look, Remy," she said, "you know I don't usually agree with a thing Kara says, and I think you should wear the LBD, OK? But it is a bit … well… All I'm saying is, no matter what he says to you, just remember this rhyme: *Play hard to get and you won't regret.* OK? Because men—"

"Are dogs. OK–aaay. I get it," I told her.

Right. Back to work.

11.30 P.M.

OMG! Robbie is the fittest, sexiest, most amazing boy ever!

He was *perfect* from the moment he picked me up and he had no idea what I'd been going through. The bloody girls at Kara's must have been discussing his "throat infection" when I took the maxi dress home, and by the time I got back he was as popular as the credit crunch.

I know they were telling me to be careful to protect me, but it was really doing my head in. And then the Feminazi made things worse by saying, "He sounds like a cad."

None of us had ever heard of the word "cad".

"That's probably because it's mainly used by the upper classes," she explained.

No. That's probably because it was mainly used 150 years ago, I thought.

But I didn't dare say that out loud. Because Kara's the same age as Madonna, and looks all right for herself (who wouldn't if they owned a beauty salon?), she likes to think she's still young.

Anyway, when she said, "A cad is probably what YOU girls would describe as a player," the girls loved it and kept saying in fake posh voices, "So, we'll finally get to meet the cad!"

I laughed it off, but I really wanted them to shut up. Especially the Feminazi. And it was like Robbie read my mind, because when he arrived he politely introduced himself to the girls and shook their hands. Then he walked me to his spanking new black Range Rover and held the passenger door open for me like in the movies. His white linen suit was spotless. His hair (with the highlights I'm going to fix) was blowing in the breeze and he looked absolutely drop-dead! But the best bit was that the Feminazi looked like she was actually about to! In. Her. Wannabe Madonna. Face.

Robbie's car is unbelievable. It has wheel rims I've only ever seen on *Pimp My Ride*, cream leather seats with his initials on the headrests, an Xbox, a DVD player and a sat-nav that's actually set IN the dashboard!

"It's a secret, princess," he said when I asked where he was taking me. And I really did feel like one – Princess Remy Louise (Wilkins) Bennet. ☺

Robbie weaved his way through rush-hour traffic and then we hit a chock-a-blocked M1, but I wouldn't have cared if it had taken for ever to get there, because he was full of banter and kept telling me how nice I looked. He had me laughing and blushing all the way, until we finally turned into a gravel drive that took us past a golf course and led us up to the front of a HUGE cream-stoned mansion.

A doorman dressed in a smart grey uniform said, "Welcome to Le Grove, madam," and it was so–oo unbelievable – him calling ME madam – that I had to fight off the giggles.

"We're eating in the restaurant," Robbie told him, getting out of the car and handing him his keys.

The restaurant was amazing, with crystal chandeliers hanging from the ceilings, and I swear it was fit for royalty. I scanned the room as we were shown to our table – gorgeous girls dressed to kill were having dinner with grey-haired old men. *He–eeeelp!* I thought, convinced they were all staring at me. Then my LBD kept riding up as I walked (which made my nerves even worse) and I had to keep tugging it back down. It was a relief when I finally made it to our table without exposing my backside to the world.

As we looked through the menu, Robbie cracked a few jokes about being the youngest bloke in the room. Then the waiter came for our order and I asked for the steak.

"Make that two," Robbie said.

SEE, he CAN read my mind. He even ordered the same food!

When he asked for an expensive bottle of wine, I wanted to down it with him so–oo badly but only had one glass, remembering the WAG Charter. (Obviously, I'm a mess after two.)

"Don't you like it?" he asked.

"Love it, but I'm … not a big drinker," I said.

He looked well impressed with that. His blue eyes sparkled for Christmas. "If I'm gonna drink all this wine, I'll have to book a room and drive home in the morning," he said.

Book a room? I thought. *Methinks you're trying to seduce me. Yes–ss. NO. Yes–ss. NO. Yes–ss – damn the WAG Charter. It's your life.*

"Do you want me for dessert?" asked Robbie.

"Huh?" I gasped.

"I said d'you want coffee or dessert?" he repeated.

Oops! (Must invest in some cotton buds tomorrow.) "Er... Yeah. Dessert. Why not?" I replied.

I had an apple tart that looked delicious, but I couldn't taste the bloody thing because every part of me was wondering what to do. From: *OMG, shall I go up to his room and just go for it?* To: *But the WAG Charter says I have to wait eight weeks!*

Aargh! Then I remembered Malibu's warning this afternoon. "Right, Remy, do you want to be his plaything for one night? Or" – I glanced up at the chandeliers, then flicked my eyes to the windows and absorbed the acres and acres of immaculate lawnage – "do you want to live like THIS for the rest of your life?"

No-bloody-brainer.

So I told myself: *Play hard to get and you won't regret.* And I did it again and again and again. Five times. Eight times. Twenty times. Until Robbie said, "You look exhausted, princess. I'll call you a cab."

He walked me to the cab, and before I got in he snogged me to within an inch of my life.

Definitely the best date in the history of the universe!

Thursday 26 June – 3.00 a.m.

I was having a proper hot dream about Robbie. Things were steaming up in the Le Grove hotel room. Then, just as it was getting to the best bit, I sprang up thinking, *OMG. He didn't even TRY to take me up to his hotel room last night. Why? Why? Why?*

I'm not saying he should have jumped on me or anything, but he could have at least attempted to get me up those stairs. Asked me up for a coffee. SOMETHING.

I think I need some moral support.

I'll phone Kellie. We're allowed to wake each other up in emergencies.

3.15 a.m.

"Do you know what bloody time it is?" Kellie moaned when she eventually answered her phone. (After my fifth try!)

"Don't get emo on me now, Kel," I told her. "Not when I need you." She listened as I told her everything. About Robbie's car. His suit. The hotel. The kiss. "Things were perfect," I said. "We even ordered the same food." Then I told her I practically had a mental breakdown deciding whether or not to go home. "But now I've clicked. He didn't want me to stay anyway." I gave a big sigh. "I dunno. Maybe he just doesn't fancy me."

"Shut up," she replied, "you're gorgeous. What did you wear?"

"The LBD."

"Hmm… LBDs can highlight your worst bits if they don't fit right, but I read the other day that a maxi dress hides a multitude of sins. Why didn't you wear that?"

Grr…

"Why didn't I wear that?" I growled. "I phoned you in the morning and asked you which dress to wear. You said you couldn't tell without seeing them."

"Sorry," she said. "But I had a little thing like AS LEVELS on my mind."

I'd totally forgotten that this was Kellie's exam week. Doh! I apologized and admitted, "I've been selfish, haven't I?"

"Yes," she said. "Can I go now?"

3.30 a.m.

I put the LBD back on to check how I looked last night and tried to think positive. *There's nothing to stop you from being the new Colleen Rooney*, I told myself. But when I swung round to see how I looked from behind, I thought, *Colleen's bum can't be this big. It just CAN'T be!* It looked like Dumbo's bum cheeks had been squashed into a piece of black cling film. No wonder Robbie couldn't wait to see the back of me. (No pun intended.)

3.35 a.m.

Can't sleep. It's weird but now Robbie's dissed me, every-thing about him seems perfect. Even his highlights and his ~~big~~ nose.

3.40 a.m.

Threw the LBD in the bin (what's the point in highlight-ing my worst bits?) then grabbed some Doritos from the kitchen cupboard (thought I might as well console myself). Was going to pig out in front of the TV, but when I opened the living-room door Dad was sleeping on the sofa. Mum always makes him sleep downstairs when she has the hump with him.

Poor Dad. We're not just joined by blood any more but by major unwantedness!

3.55 a.m.

Dear God, please let me get to sleep. I'm being assessed at the college beauty salon today and I don't want to see Robbie every time I close my eyes. Ple–eeeeease.

I'll even tidy my room.

8.15 a.m.

Typical. I finally nod off at five, then Malibu bursts into

my room three hours later to ask how it went.

"It was perfect!" I pretended. "We had dinner in a posh hotel in Hertfordshire."

"A hotel? Hmm…" she said. "I hope you stuck to the WAG Charter."

"Of course I did!" She asked me to swear on Leo DiCaprio's life. And when I did, she believed me.

"I bet he was gagging for you, though," she said.

"Yeah – had to practically beat him down with a stick."

8.58 a.m.

Right, better get ready for college. Hopefully for the last time. Can't take being a trainee for much longer. OK, so it means I get an extra hour in bed on Thursdays, but it also means that I have to do a six-day week – major sucka-tion. Plus the clients that come to the college salon think they can criticize my work just because I haven't qualified yet. Sometimes I feel like shouting, "Shut up! You're bloody getting this for free!"

Maybe I should have put up with Tara (spit, spit) Reid's bullying and stayed on for sixth form, because work isn't a bowl of cherries either. We all have to arrive looking glam and fully made-up, which takes me about an hour so I set the alarm for 7.28 a.m. (need a two-minute snooze). That's earlier than I had to wake up for school! And on top of that, I'm mainly on reception duty because a trainee is only supposed to do treatments on workmates – and the

Feminazi sticks to the rules. That means I have to answer the phone, write appointments in the diary and plaster my face with a smile like an American checkout girl – "Have a Nice Day" – the moment a client walks through the door. The Femi-nazi demands it. She says I'm the first point of contact and I'm representing her. But if I REALLY represented her, I'd stand on the reception desk and look down on everyone.

Anyway, after this session, and a good report from Kara, I should have enough accreditations for my NVQ and will officially become a beauty therapist. Ye–sss!

9.05 a.m.

Got distracted by *Big Brother*. Everyone's in bed. How can those lazy gits win 100k for this? OMG, that Bryan bloke snores like a pig!

9.10 a.m.

Strange. Lance Wilson just phoned the house looking for Malibu. Haven't heard from him in ages. I told him Malibu was at work.

"Of course," he said. "What a numpty."

He asked how she was doing and I said, "Great. She's pulled herself a Chelsea footballer." Because I wanted him to burn.

And he replied, "Great. I'm really happy for her."

Yeah, right, I thought, because he sounded gutted. Oh well, like Beyoncé says, *"If ya liked it then you shoulda put a ring on it."*

<u>9.15 a.m.</u>

Just in case Robbie didn't invite me to his room for a v. good reason (e.g. could have had hole in underpants), I've texted this message: *Thanks 4 dinner. It was great. x*

Now let's see what he comes back with. (Really wish I hadn't put that kiss on the end.)

<u>9.18 a.m.</u>

Nothing.

<u>9.21 a.m.</u>

Nothing, but won't judge. (Network could be jammed.)

<u>9.25 a.m.</u>

Still no reply.

Right, Robbie Wilkins. You are the caddiest cad in Britain. So don't even think about contacting me. No texts. No phone calls. No emails. Don't poke me on Facebook. Ever. And believe me, I'll stay strong, like other wronged women of the world, and bounce back, Jennifer Aniston and Cheryl

Cole style. Because today I WILL pass my NVQ. And that will be the first step on the ladder to me becoming a top businesswoman with salons all over the country. And you'll regret dissing me!

5.30 P.M.

College went all right today, after a proper shaky start. I did two waxes, one manicure and one pedicure, with an instructor watching me like bloody Hawk-Eye. Talk about pressure! Being emo about the Cad didn't help either. Especially when my first treatment was on Stick Insect. She may be a super-skinny model type from the neck down, but she's a horse from the neck up. I just wish she'd realize it and wipe that smug "I'm thinner than you" look off her face.

She came in for a leg wax, and grabbed a magazine to distract from the pain.

"Bloody hell," she said, flicking through a copy of *OK* magazine. "Colleen should have had another stint at Weight Watchers before she wore that bikini."

"Ah, don't be cruel," I told her. "She's gone through enough."

"See for yourself." Stick Insect pointed to a photograph of Colleen on a Barbados beach. She looked fine to me – like a normal girl who eats chips and Krispy Kremes. That's why I like Colleen. She's sort of like … me.

"Huge," said Stick Insect.

The way I was feeling, she might as well have been

prodding the flab on my bum and shouting, "Robbie reject. Robbie reject." And I remembered this time a few years ago when Malibu had looked across at a mag Mum was reading and said how pretty Steven Gerard's wife was.

"No prettier than you," Mum had told her. "You're the perfect type to marry a footballer."

I'd waited for her to tell me that I was too, but got nothing. That hurt, and it felt like Stick Insect was saying the same thing now. But there was no point in taking it out on her. I can do professional.

"Must be a bad angle," I said nicely. "Colleen's only a size ten or twelve."

"Like I said," she replied, "huge."

That. Was. IT.

While my instructor looked at the wall clock to check how long I was taking, I deliberately didn't hold the skin of Stick Insect's leg when I tore away the next wax strip. She let out a massive scream. Bloodcurdling, it was. The instructor flashed her eyes back to us straight away.

My NVQ was slipping away – FAST.

"That really hurt!" complained Stick Insect.

"Sorry, madam, is your menstruation due soon?" I said, copying the posh voice that Kara uses when she wants clients to buy an expensive product.

Luckily it was, so I told her it was a more sensitive time to wax but that I'd be doubly careful now I knew. And from the smile I got from the instructor, it looked like I'd scored some bonus marks at the same time as dishing out pain to the Stick Insect. Yay!

The only other decent thing about today is that I made up with James. He came up to me and wished me good luck as soon as I got through the college doors. So I wished him good luck too, then apologized for using his GHDs without asking, and we gave each other a big hug.

Apart from that, life is major suckeroo in Sucksville. ☹

6.30 P.M.

Malibu's home. She's just shown me a ton of soppy texts from Goldenballs, which I personally think is an invasion of his privacy. She's all Gary this, Gary that, Gary three bags bloody full.

7 P.M.

I've started writing a poem:

> *Loser, wait till you check what you've lost.*
> *You're gonna cry me a river. Yeah – why don't ya just.*
>   (Borrowed a little for that line.)
> *And when I have the number-one beauty shop,*
> *You'll be gutted about what you almost got.*

Needs a bit of work but I'm sure Miss Stevens, my old English teacher, would write "Shows great potential."

Yeah! Girl Power, baby!!

Why, oh why, oh why hasn't Robbie texted me? Is he one of those hot and cold blokes that Katy Perry sings about? Or is he just a cruel person who gets thrills out of making people feel like crap? Because I hate him if he does. And I don't want to see him again. Ever. I mean it this time. I hate being on this roller coaster. And I— Eek! Phone's ringing.

OMG. It was Robbie!! And there's been a HUGE misunderstanding. He said that when he checked out of Le Grove this morning he accidentally left his mobile in the room, and that he has an old one but my number isn't in it, so he went back to collect it as soon as he could.

And just when I was about to say, "Yeah, right," he told me he used his old mobile to call Gary and told him to tell Malibu to tell me.

Grr… Malibu does my head in sometimes.

Anyway, he apologized a gazillion times. And said that he was dying to see me again. "Will you be around tomorrow evening?" he asked.

I wanted to say, "You bet your ass I will!" But instead I said I just had to check my diary. Then I waited a few seconds before announcing, "Actually I am."

He's going to call tomorrow morning to confirm things.

Oh well, back on the roller coaster of *lurve*. ☺

Malibu just burst through my door and went, "Oh yeah, I forgot to tell you Robbie—"

"Left his phone at the hotel," I finished for her.

"Oh, you know – cool," she said.

I'd wring her neck if I wasn't so happy. ☺

8.30 p.m.

Uh-oh. I think Dad is in deep trouble. The house phone rang, Mum picked it up in the hallway and then started to hiss. All I could hear was, "And what time do you call this?" Then "Something, something, RIDICULOUS. Something, something, TAKE IT BACK."

I knew straight away that it was Dad she was hissing at. I was sitting in the kitchen snacking on Doritos, and the fact that she stomped back in when the call ended and scraped his dinner into the bin confirmed it.

He tries to finish work at six so he can be home for dinner at six-thirty, like Mum wants him to. But he says that when you have your own business, like he does with Uncle Pete – boringly called "P (for Pete) & R (for Reg) Bennet" – you can't afford to lose customers. So if he's running late because he's having a major problem fixing a washing machine or a tumble dryer, he just phones to let Mum know. Then she stores his dinner in the oven with the temperature on low.

"What d'you do that for?" I complained as Mum slammed the lid back down on the bin.

Instead of answering, Mum threw me the evil eye and stomped into the living room.

10.05 P.M.

Dad came home about fifteen minutes after Mum had chucked his dinner and headed straight for the kitchen. I was in the living room with Mum and we were watching *London Airport*.

"Remy?" Dad called.

"Yes, Dad?"

"Can you ask your mum where my dinner is, please?"

This time I threw HER the evil eye. *See, you only had to wait fifteen minutes!*

"Tell your dad that if he thinks I'm such a liar, he can find some other skivvy," Mum said, loud enough for him to hear. *A liar?* I thought, but I didn't see the point in repeating it. Didn't want to get involved, to be honest.

Then randomly Dad started to sing. Eh? *"Always look on the bright side of life..."* was coming out loud and clear as pots clattered, oil sizzled in a pan and the smell of eggs and bacon wafted into the living room.

What a wind-up.

I looked at Mum, expecting her to blow, but even though she had a face like thunder, she just kept her eyes focused on the rolling credits of *London Airport*. And three

44

minutes later, in waltzed Dad with a dinner plate in his left hand and a can of Guinness in his right.

"Ah, just in time," he breezed, cool as anything as Deborah Gordon's intro for *The Entrepreneur* began. "An entrepreneur isn't trying to make a biscuit tin the new wheel. An entrepreneur is trying to discover the wheel that everyone wants to buy."

We love this show! The contestants are cocky and positive that they're going to win the chance to run one of Deborah Gordon's businesses. But people watch every week because they're positive that Deborah Gordon is going to tear one of them "a new bum-hole", as Dad puts it.

He really loves Deborah Gordon. He even has her autobiography. He says she's as tough as old boots, like his nan used to be. I like her because she's a multimillionaire now, though she used to be piss-poor. In the introduction, she explains that at school they said she wouldn't amount to much. "They said I had a problem with authority," she tells us, then she opens her arms, the camera pans out and there's a huge glass building behind her – HER building – and she says, "Well, look at me now."

Legend.

This week a male contestant got himself into a proper pickle. And Dad shouted out the usual jokes – "He couldn't sell Coke in the Sahara" and "Might as well walk the plank now, sonny Jim" – as I giggled and Mum's face became one big frown zone.

Friday 27 June — 1 a.m.

Dad's sleeping on the sofa again.

Felt thirsty, so went downstairs to get a glass of water and couldn't resist cracking open the living-room door. Sure enough, there he was. I know he's not perfect, but Mum's such a drama queen sometimes. Still, it sounds like he called her a liar. And acted like a proper wind-up merchant when he got home, when he must have known how she'd react – *You. Sofa. For the rest of the week!*

Wonder what he thought she was lying about?

Anyway, here's hoping she wins the lottery or something, because she can have the hump for ages. She gets mardy about small stuff, too, like if someone puts cups in the plates cupboard. Everything has to be so–oo perfect. Yet she'll suddenly have this mad idea to paint the bathroom pink with purple stripes, go and do it, then complain afterwards that we should have told her not to! Talk about random.

Dad's far more logical. And less moody. Plus he doesn't make a big deal about everything. Mum went nuts when I said I was going to do a Beauty Therapy NVQ instead of A levels. She said that Dad would kill me, so I was bricking it when I told him. I was even prepared to confess that I couldn't take another two years of going to the same school as Tara (spit, spit) Reid. But all he said was, "OK."

"Is that it?" I asked.

"Why? What did you expect?"

"Dunno. Drama, I suppose. I thought you really

wanted me to do A levels," I replied.

"Well … I can't have everything," he told me.

What a dude. ☺

Robbie called at 8.15 a.m.! I went giddy as soon as I heard his voice.

He said he remembered me telling him that I leave for work at eight-thirty, and he wanted to catch me before I left.

OMG. A boy that actually listens. He's so–oo perfect!

Well, almost. We can't meet today. ☹ His mum has arranged a surprise birthday dinner for his gran and he has to be there.

"There's always tomorrow," I chirped, trying to hide how gutted I was.

"I wish," he said. "But I'm going to Ayia Napa tomorrow."

AYIA NAPA?! After that, I could hardly hear him above what was going on in my head. (Mainly: *No–ooooooooo!*)

"The boys in the team always go there before pre-season training starts…"

Ayia Napa? With a bunch of footballers? Double no–ooooooooo!

"Probably would've binned it if I'd met you sooner, but…"

Bin the sun, sea and sand, and the perfect girls in their teenie-weenie perfect bikinis? Do I believe him? Hell, noooooooooo!

47

"Remy?"

"Hmm?"

"I was just saying that I feel like I've met the perfect girl and now I'm not going to see you for a week."

"Ohhhh," I said, swooning.

"Look, I know it's a bit of a liberty, and you're a stunning girl that's probably got loads of boys chasing after you, but do you think you could hold 'em off and wait for me to take you out next Saturday?"

So I took a deep breath and tried to make myself sound casual. "Sure," I said. "See you next Saturday."

OMG. He called me the perfect girl. I have absolutely nothing to worry about. ☺

But just in case: Dear God, please, please, ple–eeeeease don't let Robbie meet a girl in Ayia Napa and I promise that I'll never bitch about the Feminazi – no, will be respectful: *Kara* – again.

6.25 p.m.

Room's tidy. ☺ Nothing to do with me and everything to do with clean-up-mad Mum. (Thanks, Mum.) It's wicked to come back to a place where the carpet is actually carpet and not knickers, bras and jeans. Especially as today was a big bag of rubbish. When I got to work, Natasha asked how my date went with Robbie. She reckons he's fit, which is a major compliment coming from Natasha, but before I could tell her that, Kara marched up and asked, "How did it go?"

I thought she was still talking about my date with Robbie. "It was amazing," I replied. "He took me to Le Grove. Have you heard of it? It's a—"

"No, I meant at the college salon," she snapped, interrupting me mid-sentence.

"Oh," I said. "Not too bad."

She arched one eyebrow and scoffed, "Not too bad? How would the world survive if we had to rely on 'Not too bad'?" As if manicuring and waxing people could solve global warming.

I just shrugged and mumbled, "Well, I suppose it's up to you now." (Meaning whether or not I pass my NVQ.)

And she replied, "Yes, I suppose *it is*." Then she turned round and trotted off on her high horse. Aargh! That Feminazi does my head in.

Oops! (Sorry, God – one last chance?)

6.35 p.m.

Dad came home on time, so I thought we'd have some normality at last, but he just dropped off his work bag and then shouted to me – not Mum – that he was going to the pub. Madness.

7 p.m.

I've been having some textual seduction with Robbie. Yay!

Robbie: *Princess I've been thinking about u all day. What you doing to me?*

Me: *Gorgeous Ive been thinking about u 2.*

Robbie: *Good.*

Me: *No. Good with a cherry on top.* ☺ *x*

Robbie: *Wish I could cancel my grans bday dinner and spend the night with u instead. x*

I've read his last message about twenty times now. And I feel like I'm floating up to the heavens every single time.

8 P.M.

Mum came in and gave me a lecture about my bedroom: "I'm fed up with it looking like a bomb site," *blah blah*. While she was having a right old rant, my phone bleeped. It was sitting beside me on the bed, so I sneaked a look: *Help! At dinner from hell. Only a hot princess can save me. x*

I giggled.

"This isn't a laughing matter!" Mum screamed like a banshee.

"I'm not laughing at you. I'm laughing at something on my phone."

"That ber–loody phone. Don't ber–loody use it again while I'm talking to you," she shouted.

"Oh yeah, that's really reasonable, Mum. So if there's some major emergency, am I supposed to ignore it?"

"What emergency? Someone's run out of mascara?" she yelled.

I couldn't think of a decent comeback, so I ended up saying something that I knew would really get to her. "Just because Dad called you a liar, don't take it out on me."

Her face went so angry, it scared me. "I've had enough of your lip, young lady!" Then she stormed off. Thank God. She looked like she'd have killed me otherwise.

8.05 P.M.

Feeling guilty about mentioning Dad. But she did push me into it.

8.30 P.M.

No more texts from Robbie. ☹
   Why does he have to go to Ayia Napa? ☹ ☹
   Phoning Kellie. Need moral support.

11.30 P.M.

Spoke to Kellie for ages tonight. Didn't realize how much pressure she'd been under with her exams. She said she'd been so stressed, her face had broken out in spots. I told her I'd believe that when I saw it.

Kellie's skin is the best. Not only is it smooth, but because she's mixed-race it also happens to be a golden brown that makes me want to rub on some St Tropez tan.

Anyway, she took her last exam today and now she's

looking forward to just chilling out. I asked if she fancied catching a film (because what with falling out with Mum and fretting about Robbie, I needed to escape) but she wasn't up for it. So I expected to have the crappiest night in ever, but sometimes my big sis is like a twenty-four-year-old version of Dr Phil (with blonde hair and big boobs). Tonight she cancelled going to see Boring Roger because she could see I was worried about something. But she knows I clam up when people ask what's wrong, so instead she said, "Know what, I can't be arsed to get done up tonight. I'll stay in. We can make popcorn and watch *Titanic*."

Titanic used to be Malibu's favourite movie, then she introduced me to it and I fell in love with it – and Leonardo DiCaprio – on the spot. As we've grown older we've sort of used it as a bonding movie. Because it makes me proper emotional, I end up telling her all the things that are on my mind, from boys to sex to being bullied by Tara (spit, spit) Reid. Then she usually gives some advice – straight to the point, no messing. So by the time Leonardo said, "Winning that ticket, Rose, was the best thing that ever happened to me," I was gagging to talk about Robbie.

"Mal," I said, "do you think it's wrong to assume that a group of lads will get up to no good in Ayia Napa?"

"Er, no," she replied. "In fact I think too bloody right they will. Why?"

"But how can you be sure?" I persisted.

"Because they're blokes, Rem. That's what they do. Now why?"

"Well… It's just… Well… Robbie's going."

"Oh, grrreat. When?"

"Tomorrow," I told her. "With some boys from his team."

"See what I mean? What did I tell you about having a back-up plan?" she said. "A fail-safe. You need bloody options."

"Yeah, but—"

"No buts," she cut in. "It keeps them on their toes, for one. And for two, it stops you from giving yourself completely – which is important."

"Why? That's not the way you treated Lance," I said.

"Yeah, and look where that got me."

She broke up with Lance a year ago, and I thought about all the boys she's gone out with since: Roger, James Murray, Garth Williams, Jermaine Dixon, Simon Taylor, Jake Kasper. And now she'll probably add Goldenballs to the list. She's a proper pulling machine. Not like me, who has only slept with one bloke who's very far from fit, one who's fit but was secretly dating my worst enemy (I hate you, Ray Pearson) and one who's only fit when he's just cut his hair.

"What d'you mean? You're happy, though," I said.

"Yeah … I am. But still. Get with it, Remy. Besides, it's not like it's gonna be hard. Even *I* can name a guy that's probably still gaga about you."

"Like?"

"Like … Spencer."

I imagined Spencer just after he's cut his hair: *Hmm.* Then I imagined him as he is most of the time, and reminded her that he'll be back off to uni in about 2.2 seconds. "Loughborough an' all. That's bloody miles away. That's why we broke up. Remember?"

"So?" she said. "You're not looking to get married. You're just making sure you can't get played. And a player CAN'T get played."

"Yeah, well, I'm not sure if playing's my thing."

"Yeah, well, maybe you should check whether Robbie feels the same way first. I don't trust him, Rem. He's a bloke, for a start. Plus I'm not into that 'leaving his mobile at the hotel' crap. That's why I reckon I forgot to tell you."

"OK. Point taken. Let's just change the subject. By the way, Lance called for you yesterday. I forgot to tell you, too."

"Yeah, I know," she said.

"And I told him you've pulled a footballer. You should've heard him. He sounded gutted. A gutted little cad," I added in Kara's posh voice, giggling.

Malibu didn't join in. She sighed. "Yeah, well, they're all the same."

"But not Roger," I reminded her, thinking: *And maybe not Robbie.*

"No, not Roger," she admitted. "That's why he's my fail-safe, but…"

"But what?"

"Nothing. You wouldn't understand."

Grr. I hate when she does that. It's like she thinks I'm still a baby or something. I understand loads. I got an A in GCSE English, for a start, and you can't do that without being good in comprehension. Fact.

"And what about Gold— I mean, Gary?" I asked.

"What about him?"

"Do you think a footballer can be good?"

"Doubt it. But he is surprising me," she said. "Some of the texts he sends are really deep. Like quotes from philosophers and stuff. So… I'll give him the benefit of the doubt."

"Really?" I said, happy because that meant Robbie deserved the benefit of the doubt too (though I must admit his texts aren't exactly deep).

"Yep," she replied. "Besides, anyone that says they want to take me to the Orchid Bar deserves it." As she said this, Malibu broke into a massive grin.

"The Orchid Bar!" I squealed. "No way!"

We'd seen so many celebrities coming out of there in all the magazines that we read, and now my sister was going to be one of them!

"When?"

"Tomorrow night."

"You're so—oo lucky," I told her.

Day Six in the dysfunctional Bennet house, and yet again Dad spent the night on the sofa. This morning I popped my head round the living-room door and asked him if he wanted a cup of tea.

"Sure, love. Why not?" he said, looking sheepish.

Didn't bank on bumping into Mum in the kitchen, though. She was up double early for Saturday shopping. Maybe she should buy some "moody knickers" tablets while she's at it. That would help everybody. Anyway, after the look she gave me when I walked in, I didn't bother to apologize for bringing Dad into our argument yesterday.

7.45 a.m.

Yay! Robbie has just texted: *Getting on the plane princess. C u when I get back. x*

He's boarding the plane but has still taken the time to text ME. He definitely deserves the benefit of the doubt. ☺

(Still not a very deep text, though.)

Just remembered Malibu's going to the Orchid Bar tonight. And the way my parents are going, I doubt they'll be off down the pub – which means that they'll stay in and ignore each other instead. I'd rather stick a hot needle in my eye than hang around their misery, so I'll text Kellie and James. One of them must have something to do tonight:

Hey guys its Saturday whats going on? Lets partyyyyyyyy.

<u>8.25 a.m.</u>

Result! Kellie has a birthday party to go to in Shepherd's Bush. (She had been just about to invite me.) And James is going to hit the bars in Old Compton Street. He says I'm very welcome to go along. Decisions, decisions.

<u>7.30 p.m.</u>

Had the day from hell and need my NVQ, pronto! Then I won't have to sit at the reception desk with Malibu at her nail station – the first one behind me – boasting about the Orchid Bar and Goldenballs all day long.

"The Orchid Bar!" the beauticians squealed when she told them she was going there first thing this morning.

"The Orchid Bar!" all her clients squealed when she broke it to them (within two seconds of them sitting down.) "Wow!"

Yes. Wow. Bloody. Wow.

I wouldn't say I was jealous, but I was definitely irritated by the way she acted like Goldenballs is perfect but never mentioned the fact that she's doing the dirty on him with Boring Roger. No. Her little fail-safe speech didn't even got a look-in. Isn't the universe supposed to punish people for stuff like that? Because I can't understand why I – the one who isn't stringing along two blokes – am coming off second while everything is going so perfectly for Malibu.

1. Why can't Goldenballs be the one in Ayia Napa and Robbie be taking ME to the Orchid Bar?

2. Why does Goldenballs play for a bigger football team than Robbie?

3. Drive a better car?

4. Text her more?

5. And why is it that even my loveliest message from Robbie will probably never compete with one of hers, because Goldus Bollockus always comes up with something deep and bloody meaningful?

I felt even more sorry for myself when Malibu's client Plastic Fantastic screeched, "The Orchid Bar? Omigod, it's so–oooo you!" when she heard the news.

"So, what does your Gary look like then?" she asked as Malibu started filing her nails.

"Oh, he's ama–aaaaazing. The spitting image of Will Smith," said Malibu. Then she stopped filing, looked towards me and said, "Isn't he, Remy?"

I thought, *this is it*. This is the universe hitting Malibu right back in her face, because Goldenballs may have a lot of things on Robbie, but he is nowhere near as good looking. In fact, even though the club was dark and I've only seen him once – and it was a week ago – I'm 110% certain that Will Smith HE AIN'T.

I cleared my throat. "Well, actually he's er … he's er…"

I could feel everyone in the salon focused on me. And Malibu was eyeballing me. HARD. Her pupils were saying,

"Back me up." Not in a threatening way. They were *begging*.

I turned to Plastic Fantastic. "He's … a … a …"

Then I caught sight of Malibu's begging eyes again.

"He's a… Ugh." I sighed. "He's a dead stamp of him. Yeah."

I just couldn't do it. Family loyalty and all that.

"Oh my god. AND a footballer," said Plastic Fantastic. Then she gave me a look of pity as she said, "Well, you never know, you could be next."

Aaaaaaaaargh! I hate being patronized!

"Actually, I'm sorted," I told her through gritted teeth.

"Oh, really?" she replied, looking surprised.

"Yes. I'm seeing Gary's mate, Robbie Wilkins. He plays for Netherfield Park Rangers," I announced.

"Good on ya, girl. So are you going to the Orchid Bar too?" she asked.

"Er, no. We can't. He's a … way." I was starting to regret opening my big mouth.

"Shame! Where's he gone?" asked Plastic Fantastic.

"Ayia Napa," Malibu answered for me, and I don't know whether she timed it deliberately, but the words left her lips just as everything and everyone had taken a pause – the phone, conversation … BREATHING.

So much for family loyalty.

"Ayia Napa?!" everyone repeated. It was obvious from their voices what they thought. That he'd cheat on me.

Cheat on me? Listen to what I'm saying – he CAN'T cheat on me because I'm not even his girlfriend. YET.

But I'm now even more worried (if that's possible). And he's there and there's nothing I can do about it. ☹

<u>8 P.M.</u>

Malibu came in to model the dress she's wearing to the Orchid Bar tonight. Can't believe she had the cheek to warn me about my LBD for the date with Robbie when her dress was so tight, you could see what she'd had for dinner!

It was also luminous orange, to match her luminous orange nails. She called it her neon look and said it's going to be big this summer.

"This is the face I'm gonna pull for the paparazzi," she said. Then she pouted her lips until they looked like Angelina's.

I must admit, she looked great. Goldenballs will be well impressed. She said she's planning on them becoming the new Posh and Becks.

Does Victoria Beckham know about this? I thought.

<u>8.10 P.M.</u>

James just called. "How ya doin'?" he asked, like Joey from *Friends*.

I ran my fingers through my hair and said, "I need a look. What about going blonde?"

He's told me time and time again that going blonde will

ruin the condition of my hair, but he repeated it one more time and said he'll work some long layers into it.

"Hmm," I said. "I was thinking … a fringe."

"A fringe will be too drastic. It's best to take baby steps," he said.

"Oh. OK." I sighed.

"What's wrong?" he asked.

"Nothing."

"Remy?"

"Nothiiing."

"Reme–eeey?" he insisted, and it was obvious he could tell something was up.

"OK," I said. "What chance do I have? Robbie's probably already had about thirty stunning girls throw themselves at him in Ayia Napa."

"But you're stunning too," he assured me.

"I'm not. And even if I was, I'm not size eight with big bazookas, am I?"

"Remy, Malibu is Malibu and you're YOU, a fabulous individual. Besides, I actually think you've got an advantage – boys like a woman with a bit of meat on her bones. Now are we zhushing it up tonight or not?"

"Um… No, I forgot I was meant to be going out with Kellie," I said.

But I actually made my decision as soon as he said "meat on her bones". What makes him think that's a compliment?! ☹

Oh well, I'll get over it. Now I'm going to phone Kel.

Dad was in the living room watching *The Bourne Identity* when I told him I was going out with Kellie.

"Great," he said. "Make sure you tell your mum."

So I then had to go to my parents' bedroom, where Mum was sitting up in bed watching a film called *The Bridges of Madison County*. (She watches that almost as much as I watch *Titanic* – and cries just as much at it too, if not more.)

"Mum, I'm going out with Kellie, OK?" I said.

"OK," she replied, snivelling. "Make sure you tell your dad."

I wanted to say, "Why don't the pair of you stop being stupid and just talk to each other?" But there was no point, I know what they're like. And it'll probably blow over by tomorrow anyway.

Right, party, here I come!

11.45 P.M.

Had an absolutely crap night. Tara (spit, spit) Reid was at the party that Kellie took me to. What a nightmare! First of all, she and her stupid friends kept blatantly pointing at me and talking about me from across the room. Proper playground stuff it was, like we were twelve all over again. Then one of them, Chelsea Braintree, had the nerve to look me in the eye and mouth "bitch".

"Just ignore them," Kellie said. But then she went off for a dance and a smooch with Taylor Metcalfe, which left me on my own feeling like a right idiot. Two boys came up to talk to me. One called Brian, who was OK, so I said he could add me on Facebook, and another called God knows what because Tara walked by and deliberately bumped into me before he could tell me his name.

"Oi," I said, "don't do that!"

"Or what?" she snapped, pushing her face right up to mine.

I was scared but determined not to show it. So I held my ground and said, "Look, Tara, what's your problem?"

"Stop playing dumb."

"I'm not. You've hated me from day one. But if you're talking about Ray – I dumped him as soon as I found out he was seeing you too."

"You dumped HIM? Who do you think you are?" she said. "The fucking queen? You ain't nothing special. With your elephantitis arse and bandy legs. Ray was using you, you stupid bitch."

I could feel tears building. And I really didn't want her to see them. So I just said, "Yeah? Well, fuck you!" and ran out.

When I hit the street, I kept running and looking behind to make sure she wasn't following. I couldn't see her or her friends, but I kept running just in case, until my heart was bursting through my chest and my feet were burning in my high heels. Then I stopped and checked how much money I had, because I'd planned to share a cab with Kellie.

I knew £5 wouldn't be enough to get me home, but I didn't want to walk or take the bus – anything could happen at that time with the nutters you get round here. So I phoned home and Dad answered. I was really crying by then.

"Dad," I sobbed, "I'm on my own in the middle of Shepherd's Bush and I haven't got enough money to take a cab back and—"

"Don't worry," he said before I could finish. "Just find a cab station and I'll pay."

Kellie rang as I got to Radio Cars.

"What happened?" she asked.

"Tara Reid, that's what," I replied. "Kel, I don't want to be within three miles of that girl."

"I didn't know she was going to be there!" she protested.

"Yeah, but you didn't exactly have my back when you realized that she was, did you?"

"Of course I did!"

"No, you didn't! You were more concerned about snogging Taylor Metcalfe," I snapped.

"That's so–o wrong," she said. "Come on, Rem, you know I've been after Taylor for ages."

"Whatever, Kel," I told her. "Just don't expect me to have your back when you're in trouble."

I knew Dad would want to know what had happened, so in the cab I made up a story about having a fallout with Kellie. There was no point letting him know that the Tara situation had been more serious than I'd let on.

Anyway, he bought it. And went back to sleep on the sofa.

I want to sleep too but I can't. I keep thinking about what Tara said about Ray using me. I'd really liked Ray. And she said I had an elephantitis arse and bandy legs. Is that what people think?

Is that what Robbie thinks?

I hate being me.

Sunday 29 June – 10 a.m.

My phone's ringing for the twelfth time in a row. I bet it's Kellie again. Don't know whether I'm ready to speak to her yet. She's...

10.05 a.m.

OK. I answered it. And Kellie apologized straight away.

"Kel, I'm already a nervous wreck about Robbie and I don't need anything else on my plate," I told her.

"OK," she said, "but I swear I had no idea Tara Reid would be there."

"I know, I know," I admitted.

Anyway, she convinced me to go to Camden Market with her. Just off to get ready.

5 p.m.

Camden was great. I bought a Shia La"Buff" T-shirt, a leather bag that has two long strings to open and close the zipper, and some earrings. Kellie bought some trainers and took two phone numbers. (What a minx!) Then we had lunch at the Loveshack, a Fifties-style American diner that has red-leather booths and a milkshake bar. Kellie ordered barbecued ribs and chips and a Double-Decker milkshake. It's the kind of thing I'd usually have, but I went for a chicken Caesar salad and a glass of apple juice instead.

"What's with the salad?" Kellie asked.

"Just watching my weight, that's all."

"If you're watching your weight, I'd better be double watching mine – with my thunder thighs."

"Yeah, right. Your legs are great. Not bandy, like mine."

She frowned. "Bandy? Your legs aren't bandy. What you talking about?"

"According to Tara Reid, they are. And apparently my arse has elephantitis."

"That's crap," she scoffed, then she sucked hard on her straw and a quarter of her Double-Decker milkshake disappeared.

"Well… I'm watching my weight, anyway," I said.

"Which is stupid if you're doing it because of Tara Reid. She's just jealous of you."

"It's not just because of her," I said.

"Well, who then? Robbie?"

I nodded. "I don't know what magazines you've been reading lately but have you seen any fat WAGs?"

"No. But then you're not fat."

"Come on, Kel, Robbie has so much choice, why would he want to be with someone who's not perfect?"

"Because she's a great girl who's perfect for HIM! And if he doesn't realize that, he can jog on," she replied.

"Hmm. Maybe Malibu's right and I should get a fail-safe to keep him on his toes."

"A what?" asked Kellie. So I explained Malibu's fail-safe theory to her. "So basically you keep the guy you DO want interested by having another guy you DON'T want on the side?" she said.

"Yep," I confirmed. "Because that way you're preoccupied, so the guy you DO want doesn't think you're really into him – which makes him want you more. But the fail-safe has to be crazy about you so that if you do run off with the one you really want, the fail-safe will take you back again if it all goes horribly wrong."

"You're sister's gangsta," Kellie said. "I like her style… But what would happen if she fell for her fail-safe?"

I thought about it for a second. "Nah. She wouldn't. Roger's so… Blah."

"But if she did, that would sort of still be perfect, right?"

"S'pose so, in a way," I said. "She reckons Spencer should be my fail-safe. But I dunno. I don't feel right about it. He was good to me. It was only him going to uni that spoilt things."

"Yeah, I see what y'mean. But if you did play them both, they'd never find out, would they? Robbie and Spencer are from two completely different worlds."

I still didn't feel comfortable about it, so Kellie said to give Robbie until 9 p.m. tomorrow evening to call or text.

"If he doesn't," she said, "you should take it as sign that he's not that into you and get back in touch with Spencer. At least then he'll keep you occupied while Robbie's away. And if Malibu's theory's right, it'll kick Robbie up the bum too. You can't lose."

I see her point. But why am I so hoping that Robbie contacts me by 9 p.m. tomorrow?!

6.30 P.M.

Well, it sounds like Malibu had a star-studded time at the Orchid Bar. She saw Simon from Blue (just as good-looking in real life), Sarah from Girls Aloud (much smaller than she thought) and JLS (those boys are everywhere).

"It's amazing. You've never seen nothing like it," she said. "And I even got my picture taken by the paparazzi!"

"No way! Did you do the pout?"

But she didn't reply because her phone rang. She answered it, then turned to me and said, "Um ... this is gonna be a long one." So I took the hint and went.

7.30 P.M.

Malibu's still on the phone. It's been an hour! I've been flicking through mags, sort of waiting for her to finish talking so she could tell me more about the Orchid Bar.

Now I feel like a right twot.

Right, that's it. I'm going to watch my DVD box set of *Friends*, and there's no distracting me once I get into *Friends*, so she can jog on.

I'll watch it in my room, though, because the living room is a war zone – Mum is sitting on the sofa on one side of the room and Dad is sitting in an armchair on the other. She has a book held to her face and he has a newspaper. The silence is deafening. (To think I'd been convinced they'd make up by today.) It's official – my family are a joke!

9 P.M.

Just watched the episode where Rachel realizes that she wants Ross and goes to the airport to meet him from China, but he arrives with a girl. Rachel looked gutted.

Come on, Robbie. You have twenty-four hours to pull your finger out!

scan the code to read Gary's texts to Malibu:

Monday 30 June — 8.05 a.m.

The phone rang at 8 a.m. and I rushed to it, hoping it was Robbie, and groaned when I realized it was Kel.

"Has he called yet?" she asked without even saying hello.

"No," I replied. "But there's still, like, thirteen hours to go."

"Bet you're bricking it, though, aren't you?"

"Kel, have you actually called for a reason or did you just want to torture me?" I asked.

"What d'ya mean?" she protested. "I woke up specially for this ... torture."

"It's not funny," I said over her giggling, but I must admit I did have a little smile on my face. I mean, who else but Kel could be that twisted?

<u>8.20 a.m.</u>

I've been looking at my naked bod in the mirror because I don't care what Kel says, Tara (spit, spit) Reid must have said those things about me for a reason. Anyway, I've decided: I need to lose weight on my bum and legs. End of.

<u>7 p.m.</u>

Staying in my room. Mum and Dad are making the atmosphere in this house bloody unbearable and I don't need it. Especially tonight. Hated every minute of being in the salon today. It was all about Malibu. Her and Goldenballs and the Orchid Bar. I think I know every detail, from the way that she posed for the paparazzi down to the colour of her knickers. Even Natasha looked impressed, and Blow-dry Sarah (whose hair, by the way, looked even bigger and fluffier than usual) said she was going to buy every magazine for the next two weeks to see whether Malibu's picture was in one of them. And she will as well. If Malibu told her to jump out of a plane, she'd do it.

Anyway, because I was so nervous about Robbie making the deadline, I kept going to the toilet to check my phone, and got a little more gutted every time I saw there were no messages. ☹

<u>7.05 P.M.</u>

PS There was one decent thing about today – I was good with foodage. Only ate a packet of crisps and an apple. And I fobbed off Mum when she offered me dinner by saying I'd have it later. I feel a little bit light-headed but that's probably just my body adjusting. I'll get used to it.

<u>7.30 P.M.</u>

Kellie just called. "Has he phoned yet?"

"How can he, Kel, if you're always on the line?" I complained.

"All right, all right, keep your hair on."

Ugh! I feel like I'm sitting here waiting when I already know how it's going to end. Robbie's not going to phone. I can feel it in my bones.

<u>8 P.M.</u>

Mum called up to tell me it's getting late to have my dinner. I shouted back that I didn't want it, so she came into my room and said, "What're you going to eat then?"

"Nothing," I answered.

"Nothing?" she barked.

"OK. Something then," I said, annoyed.

"Something like what?" she snapped.

"Something like whatever I feel like eating, Mum,

because I'm practically an adult!" I snapped back.

She glared at me and said, "This is MY house and you'd better watch how you speak to me. Otherwise, if you're such an adult, you can get up and go."

Whatever, I thought.

"Did you hear me?"

"Yes, Mum. GOT IT."

Usually she'd run off to Dad and complain about my attitude, and then Dad – the voice of reason – would come in, give me a bit of a talking-to (without ever raising his voice), then convince me to apologize. But she's burnt that bridge now – she can't look for support from someone she's relegated to the sofa.

8.30 p.m.

Half an hour away from the deadline. I'm so–oo nervous. I even knocked on Malibu's door to have a little chat, but she was having one of her marathon calls again. She'll give herself a brain tumour if she's not careful. I suppose that's what it's like when you've got two blokes.

Come on, Robbie. You've now got twenty-eight minutes and fifty seconds!

8.59 p.m.!

It's no use. Staring at your mobile, willing someone to ring it, almost guarantees that everyone under the sun will phone apart from the person you're hoping for. First, the Feminazi called to tell me to come in early (there's something she wants to discuss). Usually I'd ask a few questions – "Oh, really? Something to do with work or my NVQ?" – so I can be prepared. Tonight I couldn't get her off the phone quick enough. "Yeah, sure, quarter to nine. OK, bye."

The next person was James. "How ya doin'?"

I said, "Um … can I call you back later, babe? Please?" And I ended the call before he could answer.

Then it was Nicole Walker looking for drama as usual. "Hey, what happened? I heard it kicked off with you and Tara Reid the other night."

"I'm in the middle of something, Nic, I'll bell you back, OK?" I said.

But for all my rushing everyone off the line, still nothing from Robbie. No missed call, voicemail message or text. And I can feel myself getting angry with him, even though I know there's no logic to it because he didn't even know he had a deadline.

Eek! Phone's ringing!

9.10 P.M.

It was Kellie. "Has he phoned yet?"

"Nope." I sighed.

"Come on, Rem, at least you've got a plan B. And as things go, Spencer's quite a good plan B to have."

I explained to her that I like Spence but only as a

friend. And if I'm honest, I knew that before he went off to Loughborough, so I sort of used it as an excuse to break up.

"He was gutted enough then. Why make things worse?" I said.

"Remy, just phone the guy and see where it goes from there – and stop being so dramatic about it," she told me.

So I've just sent Spencer this text: *Hey you. Long time. Did you miss me (ha ha)? Maybe we can hook up before you go back to uni? Luv Remy x*

9.15 p.m.

Spencer called straight away and said he'd just been talking about me, which made me feel really good (see, this is what happens when somebody's into you) but also a bit guilty (I so don't want to break his heart). He asked whether I'd be around tomorrow night and said maybe we could meet up at the Milkshake Bar (our old hang-out).

"Sure," I said. "What time?" We agreed to meet at seven-thirty. But I'm still feeling a bit guilty about it.

10 p.m.

I don't get it. If I'm Robbie's "perfect" girl, why hasn't he called by now?

Doh! I know why he hasn't phoned – he's met some hot girl in Ayia Napa who doesn't have a bum that spreads from here to Timbuktu!

Right. Tomorrow I'm skipping breakfast, having an apple for lunch and then I'll see what I feel like eating when I get to the Milkshake Bar. I need bum shrinkage. And I need it right now.

Yikes! Text message!

10.04 p.m.

Only Spencer: *Really looking forward to seeing you Rem. Need to ask you something. No pressure. x*

Oh no–ooooo. Dear God, please don't let Spencer ask me to get back with him. ☹

Tuesday 1 July 7.30 a.m.

My stomach's rumbling so loud, it woke me up before my bloody alarm did. WTF?

7.35 a.m.

OMG. I didn't have dinner last night, that's why! Oh well, I'm still sticking to my plan: no breakfast.

Bum shrinkage takes sacrifice.

Nothing from Robbie. ☹

Beginning to feel glad about trying Malibu's fail-safe theory, because at least when I'm with Spencer tonight I won't be checking my phone every five seconds. It's doing my head in.

Right, I'm outta here. Need to be at work fifteen minutes early for my "talk" with the Feminazi.

6.30 p.m.

I feel awful. Weak. Knackered. Moody. Make that double moody, because only having an apple for the day is one thing but having to deal with Robbie not phoning PLUS the Feminazi is beyond punishment. Especially as our little "talk" wasn't a talk at all – she wanted me to give her a manicure. I've done treatments on all the beauticians at Kara's but NEVER the Feminazi herself. I knew she'd be judging me for my NVQ.

Don't think I would have minded any other time, but why did it have to be today, when my stomach was growling like a grizzly and my brain was 200% on Robbie?

Anyway, I knew I couldn't back out, so I did my best. And it was going well until she asked me to cut back her cuticles. I frowned. At college I've been taught that you're not supposed to cut back cuticles. You're supposed to push them back instead. The Feminazi even says it herself.

But she didn't have any dead skin, so I told her that. And it probably came across a bit aggressive because I was STARVING. (I get the right hump when I'm hungry.)

"So?" she said.

"So I don't think I should," I replied, and then realized that might not have sounded too clever either. I quickly tried to redeem myself. "Because... It won't help you in the long run – they'll only end up sticking to your nail. I'll push them ... back ... though." I started to trail off when I clicked that I was digging a bigger hole for myself. The Feminazi already knew all this – she owns a bloody salon. And from the look on her face it was obvious that there was one rule for her and another for the rest of us.

"Forget it," she said. "I'll get Natasha to finish up."

I now expect her to mark my NVQ with a big fat zero. ☹

6.45 p.m.

Even though I'm not really in the mood, I'm going to make an effort tonight (so Spencer thinks "hot" when he sees me). It calls for my dark-blue skinny jeans, my sparkly top from New Look and my Primarni mules – Blow-dry gave me a pedicure in the lunch break and I want to show off my Lush Pink toenails. If Spencer does ask me to get back with him, I'm not going to give him a yes or no answer. I'll say something open-ended, like "Let's see how things go." ☺

<u>7.10 P.M.</u>

My head's spinning. I wish it was spinning with excitement about meeting Spencer, but the truth is, I think it's because I'm so bloody hungry. And I've hardly any energy.

OMG. I need about twenty Red Bulls to feel human again.

Right, I'm going to stuff my face at the Milkshake Bar – and not with bloody salad, either.

<u>9.35 P.M.</u>

My life is a disaster movie. Right up there with *The Day After Tomorrow*, *2012*, *Armageddon* and that one about the meteor. Here's why.

I get to the Milkshake Bar and Spencer's there – so far so good.

"You look amazing," he tells me. And he doesn't look too bad himself – black jeans, blue Fred Perry polo shirt, fresh new haircut. So far so better.

The waiter shows us to a booth, we sit down, and before we've even ordered, my mobile starts to ring. I scramble around in my bag like a crackhead looking for a pipe, because I just know it's going to be Robbie. It's Murphy's Law (which Miss Stevens taught us about once in a creative writing lesson) – i.e. if things can go wrong, they will. And they bloody well did!

Anyway, I finally grab my phone, having had to take

my front-door keys and make-up bag out of the bag first, and (surprise, surprise) Robbie's name is flashing up on the screen.

"Er… Um… Um… I've got to take this call," I stutter, panicking. And before Spencer can answer, I jump up and start running to the door so I can speak to Robbie outside. (I couldn't lurve-chat with him in front of Spencer.)

But I don't even get to hear Robbie's voice. Just as I reach the door, I only go and bloody faint!

I don't know how long I was out for, but I opened my eyes to find about six people gawping down at me. I smiled when I realized one of them was Spencer.

"You all right, babe?" he asked.

"Yeah," I groaned. "My phone. Where's my phone?"

"Don't worry about that for now, love," said a balding man I'd never seen before. He was about forty, with a northern accent, and he was wearing a Milkshake Bar uniform with a badge on his shirt that said "Manager Harry Lewis". "You've … faint-ed," he said loud and slow, as if I was deaf.

Yeah, I kind of gathered that.

"Now, we'll help you to sit up slowly and see how you feel. Then we'll help you to your feet and see how you feel, and then you can decide whether you want your man here to take you to the hospital."

My man? The hospital? Why was this happening to me?! And can someone please tell me who this bloody Murphy is? Because I hate his law!

Anyway, the audience began to walk away back to their

tables as Manager Harry Lewis and Spencer helped me to sit up.

"I don't need the hospital. I'm fine," I told them.

"Do you remember what happened?" asked Spencer.

"Yeah, well, sort of," I said. "I was running to answer my phone and then… Ugh." I suddenly remembered missing Robbie's call.

"Do you suffer from low blood pressure, love?" asked Manager Harry Lewis.

"Not that I know of," I told him.

"Hmm…" he said. "Well, do you think you might have eaten something that didn't agree with you?"

I shook my head. "I've only eaten one thing today – an apple."

"What time was that then?"

"Lunchtime," I mumbled, suddenly feeling a right twot.

Manager Harry Lewis looked at his watch. It must have been about eight o'clock.

"Oh, right. That will be it then," he said, clearly relieved that my fainting had nothing to do with anything I'd eaten at the Milkshake Bar.

"A bloody apple? Is that all you've had?!" Spencer exclaimed.

When he took me home, Mum and Dad couldn't thank him enough. They made a real fuss of him. Anyway, he's just gone and I'm hoping that maybe this has happened for a reason, and Mum and Dad will make up (nothing like almost losing a daughter to bring people back together!)

and now one of them will bring me some dinner and a nice cup of tea because I need some Tender Loving Care.

<u>10 P.M.</u>

"How could you be so bloody stupid?" asked Mum. (So much for the TLC.)

"I'm not stupid," I said. "I was just so busy, I forgot to eat."

"Nonsense. You did it deliberately. Do you want to end up a bloody anorexic?"

"Anorexic?" I said, choking back a laugh. "Chance would be a fine thing."

"Right, so there you go. You're practically admitting that you WANT to be one."

"Mum, not eating for a couple of days isn't gonna make me anorexic. All right? Stop falling for the hype."

"It's HYPE until you end up in hospital. And then guess who's going to have to take time off work to look after you? You're so selfish! You can't see further than the end of your bloody nose."

I don't understand what it is with me and Mum. I knew she was only angry because she was worried about me, and I also knew I'd been stupid – it just bugged me to hear it from her. "Oh, I'm selfish, am I? Can you prove that?"

"Well," she replied, "I can guarantee that you haven't even thanked Alan for the money he gave you. And it's been over a week."

Trust Mum to pick the one thing that's actually true. Is she bloody psychic or something?

"Yeah, well … that's only because I didn't want to email him. I wanted to CALL him. And he wrote his new number in the card but YOU went clean-up mad and threw it in the bin."

"No, I didn't," she snapped.

"Who else would have chucked it?" I replied. "It's probably lying there now – UNDERNEATH DAD'S DINNER!"

"I tell you what bloody well happened," Mum shouted back at me. "Your—"

"That's enough," Dad interrupted before she could say another word. I hadn't even noticed that he was standing in the doorway, holding a plate of pasta in pesto sauce (my favourite). I was a bit embarrassed about him hearing how rude I was being to Mum. And Mum looked mega embarrassed too.

"I was just trying to get her to see how selfish she's being," she explained.

"Yes, I heard," Dad replied, looking at her with a mean look I'd never seen on his face before. Then Mum said she had some washing up to do, and when she left they both twisted their shoulders to avoid any chance of touching each other.

Wow, do they hate each other that much?

Dad stayed in my room and watched me eat every bit of my pasta. "A little bird told me that Tara Reid has been bullying you," he said.

I didn't answer. I was too busy thinking, *I'm going to kill that Kellie*.

"And trying to make you believe you're fat," Dad continued.

"I'm practically an adult, Dad. I can deal with it."

"Not by starving yourself, you can't."

I stared down at my empty plate. I knew he was right.

"I'm not letting her get away with this," he said.

I smiled, partly because he sounded like a superhero and partly because I wished I'd let him know when I was still at school so I could have seen him in action. There's nothing he can do about it now. End of.

10.30 p.m.

Malibu came into my room and gave me the Sermon Part Two.

I told her I didn't realize she cared so much.

"Well, who else am I gonna boss about if you're dead?" she joked, and we giggled for a bit.

"Anyway, I'd worry about Mum and Dad if I were you, not me," I said and told her how they can't even bear to be in the same room as each other.

Malibu shrugged. "I'm already prepared for the worst."

"Really?" I asked. "Why?"

I thought she had some inside information, but out came another Malibu theory. This one was called "They've let themselves go".

She talked about how slim and gorgeous Mum used to be when we were little. And it's true – whenever I used to watch Mum getting ready to go out with Dad, I'd think, *I want to look like THAT when I grow up*.

Now she hardly ever wears make-up, and the only time her hair looks good is when Malibu washes and blow-dries it. But even that only lasts for a day, then Mum goes back to dinner-lady mode and pulls it back into a crappy hair elastic. (Duh!)

"OK, I can see your point with Mum," I admitted. "But not Dad."

"Come off it," she scoffed. "What about the photo at Granny Bennet's house?"

I remembered the photo on our granny's fireplace. The one that made us gasp when she said it was Dad. He was muscly, with a mop of brown hair, and dressed in tight jeans with piping down the side and a black bomber jacket. You could tell he was cool back then. Then I pictured him now, leaving the house in his P & R Bennet overalls with his belly filling out the middle of them as though he's six months pregnant.

"Yeah, I see what you mean."

"Thing is," she went on, "when a man and woman let themselves go, it means they've got complacent. And THAT is the beginning of the end of a relationship."

Malibu and her bloody theories.

I hope she's wrong, because I still remember how miserable I was when Mum and Dad broke up before and

Dad moved out for a while. Can't let it happen again.

11 p.m.

Decided that now was the perfect time to email Godfather
Alan, for two reasons:

1. Mum was right and I should have thanked him for
my card and present.

2. Thinking about Mum and Dad's break-up when I
was ten made me remember that Alan played a huge part in
getting them back together. He was their mediator – which
can't have been easy, because although he was Dad's best
friend, he had to advise Mum as well. On top of all that,
Grandma Robinson (who came over most nights to give
Mum her "motherly" advice) absolutely hated him. I think
she was used to telling Mum what to do and couldn't stand
the fact that Mum was having none of it any more. But
despite Grandma Robinson's interfering, Alan cracked it –
in the nick of time, too, because he emigrated to Australia
a few days after Dad came back home.

Anyway, I've just sent him this email:

Dear Alan,

*Thanks for the card and money. I bought two lush dresses
with it.* [Thought it best not to mention throwing the LBD
in the bin.]

You're the best godfather ever,

Remy x

PS I think Mum and Dad are on the verge of splitting

up again. You were brill at getting them back together last time, but now that you're on the other side of the world I suppose that's going to have to be my job. Any suggestions? He—eeelp!!

<u>Wednesday 2 July – 7.45 a.m.</u>

Can't remember falling asleep last night. And I was that knackered, I must have slept through my alarm. Probably would have slept through an earthquake. An avalanche. An alien invasion. Everything except my text-message alert going off just now. I grabbed my phone from my bedside table and read: *Princess I tried to call last night. Holla. Robbie x*

That woke me up big time! I blitzed back a text: *Sorry, was dying to speak to u but fainted! In the middle of Milkshake Bar! Sooo embarrassing. Xx*

My phone rang straight away. "Princess, you all right?" he asked, sounding tipsy but genuinely concerned.

"Yeah, I'll survive," I said, grinning just to hear his voice.

"What caused it?" he asked.

"Um… I dunno… I think… Low blood pressure."

"Yeah? Well I'm gonna have to take care of you when I get back," he slurred.

My smile got even bigger. "Sounds like YOU'RE having a good time. You just getting in?"

"Yeah, leaving an after-hours club. But it's not as good as usual," he said. "I've got somebody on my mind. And the lads are gonna cane me for calling her."

That's what I like about him – he's got the gift of the gab but he never ever makes it sound corny.

I blushed and giggled. "Why are they gonna have a go?"

"It's just one of the rules. No phoning our girls back home. First one to break has to buy all the drinks. But you're worth it."

I blushed again. Good thing he couldn't bloody see me. Then I heard the sound of drunken lads shouting out in the background, so I told him to save his reputation and said goodbye.

OMG. "Our girls back home" – that means he's taking me seriously, right? Or am I being a mentalist?

7 P.M.

"I don't think you're being a mentalist," said Kellie. *Yay!*

"But…" she continued, "I don't think you should get your hopes too high, either."

I came crashing back down to earth.

We were in Nando's because Kellie had decided to meet me for lunch – which was a big honour, seeing as her life has been one big sleep-in since she took her last AS exam. (Why, oh why didn't I stay on for sixth form?) I reckon she was just trying to make sure I ate something. (Probably hired by my dad.) But there were no worries there – I couldn't wolf down my peri-peri chicken fast enough.

Kellie bit a chunk out of her half chicken extra hot and

said, "Damn, I love this shit," then turned her attention back to me. "I mean, you know what boys are like," she went on between chews. "They'll say anything to get us weak and then before you know it, our knickers are ankle-warmers."

"Speak for yourself!"

"You know what I mean, though, don't you?" she said.

Yeah, I thought, *that there are plenty of Ray "user" Pearsons out there.* I knew exactly what she meant, but it didn't mean I liked it. All I want is for Kellie or Malibu to be positive about Robbie. Just ONCE. I know what they're thinking: *He's a footballer, he's in Ayia Napa, he could charm paint off walls.* But I don't want to hear it. Sometimes it would be nice to repeat something he's said to me and not have it be torn apart or made out to be a lie.

I didn't say that to Kellie, though. Instead I said, "Anyway, forget about Robbie, you big GRASS." And I watched her squirm as she tried to justify telling Dad about the drama with Tara (spit, spit) Reid.

It basically came down to her being worried. So I forgave her. Then we spoke about Spencer for a bit and I told her I was confused because of the way he looked after me last night.

"But I just don't fancy him," I finished.

And by the time she'd explained why I should string him along anyway, it was time for me to go back to work.

I'm going to get Malibu's opinion on having Spencer as my fail-safe one more time. (Even though I'm 99% sure what she's going to say.)

Malibu had her back to the door when I walked into her bedroom. She was wearing the killer red dress that we call the Boy Magnet. So I said, "Bloody Nora, where's he taking you this time?" Assuming that Goldenballs was treating her again. But she spun round like a demon and thrust her finger to her lips, and that's when I noticed she was on the phone – she was using the loudspeaker and talking into it walkie-talkie-style.

She pressed the button to end the loudspeaker mode, put the phone to her ear and said, "OK, then, see you in about twenty minutes," in a girly voice I haven't heard her use since I can't remember when. But it instantly changed once she'd ended the call. "KNOCK BEFORE YOU COME IN MY ROOM. ALL RIGHT?"

So I stormed straight back out in a huff. And now she's gone out without even apologizing!

8 P.M.

I bloody hate living here at the minute. My sister's a schizo, and as for Mum and Dad – well, Dad hasn't even come home from work yet. And it sounds like he hasn't called to let Mum know where he is, either, which means: (a) they're still not talking, (b) he wants to bring on World War bloody Three, or (c) both of the above.

What he doesn't know is that Mum didn't make him

dinner anyway, which technically means she declared war first.

I think I'm more adult than all of them put together.

<u>8.15 P.M.</u>

Spencer just called. He asked me how I was feeling. And I think hearing his concern felt especially good because Malibu had just treated me like crap. Anyway, whatever the reason, it made me like him a bit more.

"Much better, thanks," I told him.

"OK, then let's try this again," he said, "as I didn't have a chance to ask you what I wanted to last night. What're you doing tomorrow? And I promise that this time I won't be taking you to the Milkshake Bar." He chuckled.

But I didn't laugh. I took a deep breath and said, "Spencer, I can't do this. I don't think it's right."

I made a big speech – from my heart, but if I summed it up, it was basically the old classic "It's not you, it's me." And I ended up telling him that I really wanted us to stay friends.

He said he'd have to think about it. And sounded really pissed off.

<u>9 P.M.</u>

Now I definitely know my parents' marriage is doomed. Because not only did Mum come into my room and apologize

91

for being hard on me when I fainted, but before she left she turned to me and said, "You know I love you, don't you."

LOVE?! Mum doesn't do that Disney stuff.

This can only mean one thing: Dad isn't coming home. 😞

Thursday 3 July – 3 a.m.

Dad's here – yippee!

Don't think I've slept a wink. Been lying in bed, waiting to hear his key in the door. (Which is why I heard Malibu waltz in at about one.) Anyway, he's set up camp in the front room – and I can tell he's drunk because his footsteps sounded like this: one and ... two, two. One, two... Two ... two. How does he think he's going to help the situation with Mum by turning up plastered? I'm so–oo angry with him for being so dumb, but mostly I'm just happy that he came home – I was really beginning to think he wouldn't.

Which reminds me – must check whether Godfather Alan has got back to me with some "mediator" advice.

3.05 a.m.

No, nothing from Alan. 😞

7.29 a.m.

Grr. Alarm just went off, but it's college today – forgot to reset it for my extra hour. Fixed it: now back to bed. Yay!

Grr. I'm losing it. Did my last college session last week. That means I have a day off! Can do whatever I want at last. Right, back to bed again. ☺

Changed my Facebook status to: *Remy Bennet is chillaxing.* ☺

Been lounging in my PJs all morning. Feels good but it also means I've had a lot of time to think and fret about: (a) Robbie still being in Ayia Napa, (b) Mum and Dad possibly breaking up, and (c) Spencer. What sucks the most about the Spencer situation is that not only have I dumped my back-up plan, but it looks like I'm going to lose his friendship as well.

Just hope you're worth it, Robbie Wilkins.

Kellie just called. I decided to tell her about Spencer straight away but I don't think she heard a word I said. I realized her mind was on something else as soon as I got no reply to "I know you probably think I'm stupid for not taking your advice…"

Most people (with a heart) would have tried to make me feel better by replying along the lines of: "No, of course you're not stupid."

I just got silence.

"D'you know what I mean? Kel?"

"Yeah, yeah. Don't worry about all that. I've got the answer to all your problems," she finally answered.

ALL my problems? I thought. *What, is she going to make Spencer not hate me, get Mum and Dad back on track, plus make sure Robbie doesn't meet a girl in Ayia Napa? Perfecto!*

"I'm all ears," I told her.

"One word," she replied. "The gym."

I tutted. "First of all, that's TWO words, Kel. Second of all, have you listened to a word I've said?"

"Of course I have," she said. "But I must admit, I've been more focused on the big picture. Which is: you hate your bum, I hate my thighs, now what are we gonna do about it?"

"Where're you going with this randomness?"

"I tell you where I'm going – no, where WE are going. We're going for a free personal training session at Canon's tomorrow morning." She announced it as if I'd won the bloody lottery.

I'd usually thank someone for doing something so considerate, but I know Kellie too well.

"Who is he, Kel?"

"What's wrong with you? Why've you got to be so cynical?"

"I'm not going unless you tell me who he is," I insisted.

She gave a big sigh. "Ugh, all right then. I spotted the

buffest boy on the planet yesterday, straight after I left you at Nando's. I'm talking muscles on muscles. So I speeched him – of course."

"Of course."

"And it turns out he's a fitness trainer. So guess what I said?"

"What?"

"'I'd love to have a session with you.' Get it? SESSION!"

"Duh. You don't need to explain," I replied.

"But I wasn't selfish, Rem. When he agreed, I told him that I wanted to bring a friend."

"And I suppose he's bringing a friend for me, is he?" I asked sarcastically.

"NO. I swear. It's just going to be us two," she said. "And him."

I groaned.

"Come on," she urged. "He says they've got machines that can tone us up in twenty minutes. TWENTY MIN-UTES! Even if you don't like it, at least you'll be looking tight for when Robbie gets back."

Kellie knows how to play me so–oo well. "Oh, all right then. I'm in," I told her.

1.30 P.M.

Posed in the mirror to see what I'll look like after my gym session. I turned to the side and clenched my bum in tight. Then even tighter. Fantastico! (Even if I say so myself.)

Watched a *Jeremy Kyle* repeat on ITV2 called "Fifth show, fourth girl … second DNA test!" Really cheered me up. I don't have problems. THOSE people have problems.

6.35 p.m.

I was in my room and Malibu was in hers (gassing on the house phone) when Mum called us for dinner at six-thirty on the dot. She said we have to eat together as a family, but Dad wasn't even home yet. So I did something sly. I told her that Dad couldn't get through to the house phone so he sent me a text to say he was running late.

"He asked us to wait for him," I added.

"Really?" she replied, surprised.

I know it was wrong, but someone has to do something to salvage their marriage. Anyway, I've got a plan but first I'm just going to check if Godfather Alan has got back to me. (He might have a better idea.)

6.40 p.m.

No. Still no email from Alan. I'll have to solve this parental marriage crisis on my own.

Here's the plan: the dinner Mum's just made is destined for the fridge because I'm going to blow a massive chunk of my wages and get my mum and dad's favourite food from Wong Man Chu delivered to our house. (They always go there for their anniversaries, and this will remind them of the love they can't afford to lose.) Perfecto!

But first I have to get Dad home.

6.50 p.m.

I called Dad and told him to hurry home because I needed to speak to him. Now, as lies go, technically that wasn't one, because I needed to get him to pretend HE ordered the Chinese takeaway to win Mum back.

He was umming and ahhhing about when he'd get here, so I got emotional and made out it had something to do with Tara (spit, spit) Reid. Technically, as lies go, that was a humongous fat one. But sometimes you have to do what it takes.

I'm about to place the order with Wong Man Chu and get them to deliver the food at eight. Yay!

7.30 p.m.

I've had a proper heart-to-heart with Dad.

"Dad," I said, "you and Mum have got complacent. And THAT is the beginning of the end of a relationship."

He nodded like he was majorly disappointed with himself and then said, "So I take it Tara Reid isn't about to kill you?"

"Erm … no," I admitted. "Sorry about that. I just wanted to—"

But before I could tell him about my plan he said, "Remy, you know I love you, don't you."

The "L" word AGAIN. What's got into my parents?

"Dad, are you sick or something?" I asked him.

"No, don't be daft!" he said.

"OK. Is Mum?"

"We're as fit as two fiddles," he assured me.

"Oh. Well then… In that case… Yeah, I er … love you, too."

After that he looked even more embarrassed than me. He dropped his head, shuffled his feet about and then eventually said, "Look, I know how special your half-birthdays are. So … I'm sorry for throwing away your card from Alan, OK?"

"YOU?" So clean-up-mad Mum was telling the truth! Her nagging must have turned the man she says is allergic to the Hoover into clean-up-mad Dad!

"Yes. I was having a little…" He stopped.

"Personality transplant?" I nearly said.

"Anyway, I'm sorry," he told me, then turned on his heels and scarpered.

7.58 p.m.

My (well, Malibu's) little complacency speech must have worked a treat, it sounds as though Mum and Dad

98

have made up – I can hear them kissing in the hallway. Eugh! There should be a law against hearing your parents snog!

The front door's opening. Yes–ss! This must be the Chinese takeaway arriving, to make their night even better.

I can't resist having a look.

<u>8.01 P.M.</u>

It wasn't the Wong Man Chu delivery man at the front door. My loved-up parents had opened it for themselves and were about to step out.

"Where're you going?" I asked.

"I'm taking your mum out for dinner," Dad said. "She deserves it."

"Oh, Reg." Mum sighed.

Just then, the delivery man did arrive. He got off his moped and walked up the path with four white plastic bags in his hand. "Delivery for—"

"Me!" I screeched quickly.

"Bloody hell, Remy. You feeding the bloody five thousand?" said Dad.

"Er … something like that."

Then Mum took Dad's arm and they went off like a pair of lovesick teenagers.

That's most of my wages down the drain. But solving parental marriage crisis does make me feel warm and fuzzy inside. ☺

Friday 4 July – 7.10 a.m.

Aa–aaargh, my stomach! It feels like I've swallowed a boulder. A boulder that was airlifted from the bottom of Lake Grease. OMG. Why couldn't I resist that Chinese? It was a three-course meal for two that was meant for my blooming parents and I still managed to stuff most of it!

Oh well, I'm minutes away from the personal training session that Kellie sorted out. I'm sure I'll run it off.

7.20 a.m.

Tracksuit? Check! iPod shuffle? Check! Work clothes? Check!

Right, ready to – ugh! My stomach again. Need the loo!

7.25 a.m.

OMG. I look paler than a goth. I'll have to sack the training.

7.27 a.m.

Eek! Just remembered Kellie said I'd have a toned bum in twenty minutes.

Robbie's back tomorrow – I want his eyes to pop out of his head when he sees me. Definitely have to go. How bad can it be?

Disaster! No, an absolute shameful catastrophe. It was so bad that Kevin, our trainer (who was just as fit as Kellie said), has sent me home to "recuperate".

"Don't worry, it happens sometimes," he told me.

How could he be so nice to someone who had just covered him in projectile sweet-and-sour prawns?

Oh no. I'm cringing just thinking about it.

I didn't even get to use the machine that would have toned me to within an inch of my life. What's wrong with me? I'm a disaster if I don't eat and a disaster if I do.

9.00 a.m.

I was going to take Kevin's advice and stay at home to recuperate, but then I realized that he thinks I threw up because I'd overdone it, rather than because I'd stuffed my face with Chinese food last night. So I've rushed to get ready for work. Just about to phone the Feminazi to let her know I'll be half an hour late. I'll say it's because of women's problems. Need to play my cards right to make sure she gives good marks for my NVQ. ☺

9.10 a.m.

Well ... I'm still home. There's been a change of plan and it's Kellie's fault. When she called to check how I was

101

doing, I was about to phone work.

"I'm OK," I told her. "Just proper embarrassed."

"I would've come home with you," she said, "but I thought it would be bad if both of us dropped out."

"Yeah, right. I know exactly why you didn't drop out ... KEVIN."

She started to giggle. "Busted. He's fit, though, isn't he?"

"Yep," I admitted.

"He'll show you around again when you're up to it," she told me. "And you never know, he might be mine by then."

"I bet he will." I laughed.

Kellie's amazing. She never misses an opportunity. While I stand there, willing a fit boy to come over and talk to me, Kellie's like an Exocet missile – she seeks and destroys. And it's not like she needs to do the chasing, either. To go with her perfect brown skin, Kellie has hair that drops down to her shoulders in big black spirals and the cutest little freckles running across her nose. She's so–oo pretty.

"Anyway, I'm going shopping. Coming?" she asked, interrupting my thoughts.

"I can't piss Kara off. I'm still waiting for my NVQ."

"Come on, you've got the perfect excuse."

"I feel better now, though."

Then I looked out of the window. Yep, still sunny. The kind of day that rips out your heart when you're stuck at a boring reception desk.

"Well... I suppose I DID throw up," I added.

"Uh-huh. Which means technically you ARE ill."

"And it was at the gym, so there'll be witnesses, won't there?"

"Exactly. Shall we say eleven o'clock?"

All I have to do now is phone the Feminazi and pull an Oscar-winning sickie.

9.20 a.m.

Aa–aaaarghhhh! Will somebody please put Kara Feminazi Cooper out of her misery? There's something seriously wrong with that woman. Why does she have to be so sarky? Suppose I really did have the first signs of swine flu?

OK, I exaggerated an ickle bit – but only because I knew that if I'd told the truth, she'd come up with a story like: "My grandmother, the late, great Kara Cooper the Second, broke two legs and an arm, and still carried on working through the Blitz."

Whatever. Please just give me my NVQ and go away.

Actually, she's done me a favour. She's highlighted the fact that I don't want to work for her for the rest of my life. I want to be my own boss, in my OWN beauty salon. And even though it's probably ages away, I'm going to start a business plan right now. I can look at it whenever she does my head in and think, *It's only a matter of time.*

9.35 a.m.

Er ... what does a business plan actually look like?

Google to the rescue.

10.00 a.m.

Grr. This is driving me mad! Hundreds of sites came up saying I could download a business plan sample. *Perfect,* I thought. But I don't understand a bloody word of any them. They're full of terms like "gross margin" and "quantify your market". WTF?!?!

I'm going to take a break and update my Facebook photos instead.

10.30 a.m.

Aha! Godfather Alan has finally emailed back.

Hey Remy,

How are you? Glad you liked the card. Are things any better there now?

Alan x

Wow. He's later than late.

10.33 a.m.

I replied straight away:

Hi Alan,

I'm fine. You'll be glad to know that Mum and Dad are no longer at war. Early days, though. You know what they're like.

You're still the best godfather ever, even though you took for ever to email back.

Love Remy x

<u>10.35 a.m.</u>

Alan's reply:

Stopped arguing? Do you think that's it, or are they likely to start again?

From best godfather ever, who's very sorry about late response. x

<u>10.36 a.m.</u>

I sent:

Is the Pope Catholic?

R x

<u>10.37 a.m.</u>

Alan's reply:

It's a shame they can't get on. Hope you're not too upset. I remember how badly you took it last time. Do you have someone to talk to?

Alan x

I hate being patronized!

<u>10.38 a.m.</u>

I'll live! Happen to be seventeen now – practically an ADULT.
Remy

<u>10.39 a.m.</u>

Alan's reply:
Yes, of course. I suppose I'm treating you like the ten-year-old you were when I last saw you. Forgive me. Time goes so fast.
A x

Ah, now I feel guilty. I'll write something nice.

<u>10.40 a.m.</u>

I sent:
You're forgiven! Anyhoo, how are you? Been sunning yourself? Having barbies and plenty of tinnies? (Ha, ha!)
R x

<u>10.42 a.m.</u>

Alan's reply:
I take it "Neighbours" is still big out there! Actually, been doing all of the above. But I've had seven years of it now and I'm missing home. Seriously thinking about coming back.
A x

<u>10.43 a.m.</u>

I've just sent:

When? When? When?!

R x

<u>10.44 a.m.</u>

His reply:

Pretty soon.

A x

PS Please don't tell your parents. I want to surprise them.

Yippee! I'm so happy Godfather Alan's coming back but a tiny part of me is thinking, *Oh no, I'm rubbish at keeping secrets.*

<u>3 p.m.</u>

I met Kellie at Westfield. That place is so–oo massive. Still takes my breath away. It was full of loafing sixth-formers because most exams are over. Kellie charmed a sales assistant in the Apple store and he gave her a pink silicone iPod case! Another one was eyeing me up and Kellie dared me to work some magic on him. He was cute-ish but I just haven't got it in me. Besides, I'm saving myself for Robbie. ☺

I bought some lip gloss from MAC, and Kellie bought some gladiator sandals, then we just mooched around for a couple of hours until Kellie had to go off to an interview for a Saturday job in Topshop. She's been working in Superdrug up until now, so this is a massive step up.

"You'll get it," I told her when she said she was feeling nervous. "Use the same skills that just got you a new iPod case."

Been home for over an hour now and I'm bored. Bored. BORED. Daytime TV's crap and they keep muting the sound on *Big Brother*. So–oo annoying.

Never thought I'd say this, but I actually wish I'd gone to work today. I think I've missed the laughs we have. I've even missed Malibu boasting about Goldenballs – how duh is that?

I'm going down the newsagent's. Flicking through mags will be far more entertaining.

3.30 P.M.

OMG. I have the juiciest gossip ever. I cut through the park on the way back from the newsagent's and saw Lance Wilson kissing a girl on a park bench. Not just any girl – AMY FITZGERALD! He should be ashamed of himself. He's gone from dating my beautiful big sister to publicly snogging the local bike. (The same local bike that he used to call ugly whenever Malibu accused him of fancying her.)

Well, he obviously doesn't think Amy's ugly any more, because he was so into her that he didn't even notice me. I was really tempted to say something, or at least to stand behind them and start clearing my throat: Ahem. Ahem. AHEM. But it started to rain – this country's so–oo random. And I only had a little summer dress on, so I ran the rest of the way home.

Anyhoo, I bought four magazines and I'm going to scan through them to find a look that rocks for my date with Robbie tomorrow. But first I'm going to phone Malibu to tell her about Lance and Amy. This is going to be the bitch-fest of all bitchfests!

7 P.M.

I'm so stupid! Watching *Home and Away* with Mum earlier reminded me about Godfather Alan coming back, so I blurted out, "Alan's mad to want to—"

I was going to say "come home" but I quickly stopped myself when I remembered it was SUPPOSED TO BE A SECRET.

"To want to what?" asked Mum, frowning.

"Um…" It felt like it took twelve hours to dig myself out of the hole. "Um… To want to … stay in Australia when he could be in rainy old England. Ha, ha!"

The Jedi mind trick must have worked because Mum just looked out the window, saw the rain lashing down and sighed. "Yeah."

Phew!

It's official. I have the biggest mouth ever. I've already told Malibu that Godfather Alan is coming back. And I didn't even mean to, it just fell from my lips.

"When?" she asked.

"He said pretty soon. But don't tell Mum and Dad. He wants to surprise them."

"Why?"

"Dunno, but don't tell. Ple–ease…"

I feel an ickle bit like a traitor now, but I don't think she'll tell. Malibu usually takes everything in her stride. Even me catching Lance and Amy snogging in the park didn't turn into the bitchfest I thought it would. I expected Malibu to be spitting blood, but there was a long pause and then an ice-cold "Whatever".

She's another level.

7.20 P.M.

Mum didn't cook today – she's meeting Dad down the gastro pub.

Before she left she started to say, "I stored last night's dinner in the fridge. Are you all right to…?" But she got a text before she could finish. She read it straight away and I reckon it was a romantic message from Dad, because she broke into the biggest smile ever.

"Nuke it?" I finished for her. "Course I am, Mum."

"OK then. See you later." She was positively glowing.

It's nice to know Dad can still make her feel that good, even after their arguing. Anyway, I thought it was a good time to give her some advice. Not the complacency speech – Mum wouldn't have appreciated it like Dad did – so I just said, "Mum, please drop the hair elastic. You look so much better without it."

She rolled her eyes but smiled and did it. Her hair dropped to her shoulders – blonde and not perfect, but so much better than before. Next time I'll work on her letting me make her up. ☺

7.30 p.m.

OMG. Malibu isn't as unflappable as I thought. She's having a massive barney with someone on the phone. Swearing and everything! I don't think I've ever heard her like this. Wonder who it is…?

Just overheard "messing me about". Goldenballs? It must be Goldenballs. Maybe he's changed his mind. (He's supposed to be taking her to dinner tomorrow.)

OMG, they're not golden after all – they're paper. Tee-hee.

OK, I shouldn't be so happy about it. But I'm only human and I can't help it after everyone has been so horrible about Robbie.

She's stopped now.

I'll give it five, then go and investigate.

Went into Malibu's room, looking concerned.

"What's the matter?" I asked. "Is it Gary?"

She shook her head.

"Who then?"

She didn't reply.

"Roger?"

She gave a long sigh. "Yeah, Remy … it was Roger."
Then she grabbed her (fake) Ugg boots from on the floor
beside her bed and began to put them on frantically.

"Where you going?"

"To bloody sort things out," she said, then she was off
out of the door.

8 P.M.

I'm all alone. ☹

I wonder what Robbie's up to? I bet he's in a club
somewhere.

8.01 P.M.

Bet he's in a club with his mates having a few drinks.

8.02 P.M.

Bet he's in a club with his mates having a few drinks and

some girls are trying to flirt with him.

8.03 P.M.

Bet one of those bloody girls has waited for him to get drunk and has thrown herself at him and is about to kiss him RIGHT NOW.

Grr. I'm going to call him to interrupt her evil plan!

8.05 P.M.

He answered! Couldn't hear him very well (music was too loud). He said, "Remy, listen to this," and must have held his phone towards the speakers because all I heard next was Tinchy Stryder telling me I was Number One.

The call ended and a few seconds later a text came up saying: *C u tomorrow princess x*

I love him so—oo much. Can't wait to see him tomorrow! ☺

scan the code for extra content

Saturday 5 July – 6.15 a.m.

Up double early today. Must be excitement, because as soon as I opened my eyes I got butterflies about seeing Robbie. Can't wait! Wish I could fast-forward to tonight. ☺

6.30 a.m.

OMG. Malibu's just creeping in after "sorting things out" with Boring Roger. He obviously isn't as boring as I thought. ☺

8.15 a.m.

Robbie just called!

"Princess," he said, "just landed. Fancy the cinema tonight and then a bite to eat?"

Yes—ss times two thousand!! I thought. "Sure, why not?" I replied.

This time I'm meeting him there. (Don't want him to come to the salon and feel the girls' negativity.)

6 P.M.

The first thing I noticed when I got home is that the skirting boards in our hallway had been painted in black gloss (they used to be a matt white). It looks terrible and I know Mum's the culprit but I'm saying nothing. She can bite someone else's head off for a change.

Besides, I happen to be in a v. good mood. The Feminazi made a sarky comment about my "miraculous recovery" when I got into work today, so I decided to get my head down and work double hard. I smiled in a "Have a nice day" way when clients came through the door, answered the phone in my sweetest poshest voice, ran every coffee shop errand as if my life depended on it and still managed to reshape Malibu's eyebrows in our lunch break. Basically, if I was running a salon, *I* would have employed me.

I even managed to revamp the booking system. The appointment times and names of the beauticians are always written in black biro and it can take a while to see who's free at a certain time, especially when a customer requests a particular beautician. It's been bugging me for ages. So I decided to make things clearer by giving every beautician a colour code. I even ran to the shops and bought one of those pens that has four different colours in it.

Malibu's name and appointments will always be written in blue, Blow-dry Sarah's in black, Natasha's in red and Kara's (who occasionally still does treatments when we're uberbusy) in green. Now, if someone phones and asks when Natasha's free, I can just follow the red ink and see in no time. It's genius and I'm hoping it will make the Feminazi give me extra marks for my NVQ. ☺

6.30 P.M.

Dad's just come through the front door and gasped, "Bloody hell!"

Methinks he doesn't like the black-gloss skirting boards. ☺

"What do you reckon?" Mum asked. "I got the idea from *Jazz Up Your Home*. It's a new programme on Living."

"Er… Yeah. It looks great."

Poor Dad. I'd lie too if I knew that telling the truth would have me sleeping on the sofa.

6.50 P.M.

I've changed date outfits about four times!

Now going to rock the casual sexy look – black jeans with my Primarni mules and my tight "I Dig Dead Guys"

T-shirt (sneaked some chicken fillets in my bra to make boobage look good too).

I'm so–oo excited I could barely do up the buttons of my jeans (jangling hands) but apart from that I'll survive. Aa–aaaaaaaaaaaargh!

7.20 p.m.

"Does my bum look massive?" I asked Malibu. (Couldn't leave the house without checking what she thought.)

"You're not starting that anorexic stuff again, are you?"

"Come on, stop having a laugh. What do you think?"

"I think you look great," she told me, and sounded like she meant it too. She actually looked quite happy for a change. And she was done up like the vamp Sandy in *Grease* (black shiny leggings, high heels and the red Kate Moss top that she wears without a bra, even though she knows it drops down all the time to reveal mega cleavage – what a minx).

I guessed that whoever she was going out with tonight must have been the one she liked the best.

"So, who is it tonight then?" I asked. "Roger or Gary?"

"What are you, the CID?" she snapped.

That girl's got major issues.

Anyway, who cares? Robbie, here I come!!

Sunday 6 July – 12.15 a.m.

Ama–aaaaazing night! We went to see *Action Movie Part*

II. Didn't see much of the film, though – too busy having a tongue-fest (tee-hee.) Then we went to a Lebanese restaurant called Maroush, on the Edgware Road. They do the best chicken kebab I've ever tasted in my whole life!

Robbie looks even better with a tan. And whenever his big manly hands touched me, I melted. That's why it was so hard to keep strong when he dropped me home and asked if I was sure I didn't want to go back to his place.

Believe me – I really, really wanted to. But I stuck to the WAG Charter because it's worked perfectly so far.

"Um… Maybe next time," I told him.

<u>10 a.m.</u>

I was lying in bed, thinking about Robbie, but before I knew it Spencer flashed into my head. Feel a bit guilty, I suppose. I did sort of use him. I admit that I don't deserve it, but why can't he just call and say we can be friends? I love Spencer's friendship. He makes me laugh and we like the same films and everything. In fact, in an ideal world, I'd probably take Spencer's personality and inject it into Robbie's HOT body.

OMG, Robbie looked amazing last night. His hair was perfectly gelled, his white trainers were practically gleaming and his shirt and jeans didn't have one crease. He's physical perfection. He also happens to be passionate (especially when he was talking about wanting to earn as much as John Terry). He's what I want, I know he is. And if Spencer isn't willing to be just friends, I'll be gutted but I'll have to accept it. As Dad says, I can't have everything.

Unlike Malibu Amanda Bennet, who seems to have the world at her feet! She came in at six o'clock in the morning AGAIN. And unless she's broken her own rules and spent the night with Goldenballs (which I doubt very much), it means that she decided to spend a second night on the trot with Boring Roger. WTF?!

Maybe she's fallen for him.

5 p.m.

Robbie has sent a blaze of texts saying that I'm gorgeous, sexy and hot. OK, they might not have been deep and meaningful, but they made me feel GOOD. And that's all that matters.

Someone's at the door. Maybe Mum's forgotten her keys. She went to get some white paint to restore the skirting boards to their original colour (after having a right go at us for not telling her that the black gloss looked ridiculous – duh!).

Please someone go and get it. I'm watching *Friends*.

Dad's calling me. I'd better go and see what he wants.

5.40 p.m.

OMG. I went downstairs and standing there in our hallway was Tara (spit, spit) Reid, flanked by her big fat mum! Mrs

Reid must be about twenty stone. And her face was sunburnt and sweaty.

I had no idea what they were doing there. I looked at Dad, then I looked at Tara's mum, then I looked at the floor. (I couldn't look at Tara – she psyches me out too much.)

"I think my Tara 'as sometin' to tell ya," Tara's mum said in an Irish accent. "Dontcha, Tara?" she growled, glaring at her daughter.

Tara looked like she wanted the ground to open up and swallow her whole.

"Dontcha, Tara!" her mum repeated.

And that's when Tara (spit, spit) Reid, meek as a mouse, looked me in the eye and mumbled, "I'm sorry."

"Louder!" boomed her mum.

"I'M SORRY."

Just then, Malibu came out of her room and asked, "What's going on?"

Dad put a finger to his lips.

"Now," Tara's mum said to me, "I've made sure ya da knows how to get hold o' me on my mobile and email." She pointed at Tara. "So if SHE so much as texts ya sometin' untoward, you forward it to me. If you don't like the way she feckin' looks at ya, let me know and I'll give her what for."

I know she was being nice, but Tara's mum was even scarier than Tara!

"OK. Thanks, Mrs Reid," I said.

"A quiet word, please," Tara's mum said to Dad, and they went into the kitchen. I could hear her apologizing and saying that Tara had been having a hard time about something, but I couldn't take it all in because I was too chuffed – Tara Reid apologizing to ME. And all because of Super Dad (tee-hee)!

I watched Tara standing, shoulders slumped, humiliated, in our hallway, and I didn't even feel a little bit sorry for her.

Just before Dad and Mrs Reid came back out of the kitchen, Malibu stepped up to Tara and hissed something in her ear. And funnily enough I heard that loud and clear: "You mess with my sister again and I'll knock your head off."

I really love Malibu sometimes. ☺

7 p.m.

Malibu asked me to twirl her hair with the straighteners (I do it better than she does) because she was going out. I was dying to find out who with this time, but I felt funny about asking because she's been snapping my head off every time I do. I hoped she'd slip up, or tell me, but she kept the conversation strictly on Tara Reid (Tara's face when her mum shouted at her, Tara's face when she had to say sorry to me, Tara's face when Malibu threatened her…). We had a right laugh about it.

When I finished her hair, she posed – "Ta-dah!" Her make-up was flawless and her mascaraed lashes were so long, they could have been spider legs framing her blue eyes. But most of all she looked happy and relaxed, so I thought what the hell and asked if she was going out with Goldenballs tonight.

"What makes you think that?" she said with a smirk on her face.

"Because you've made a proper effort."

"Oi, I always do, you cheeky thing!"

Something about the way she said that made me think I was wrong. "Roger then?" I asked, and she went dead quiet.

BUSTED! I thought, because tonight would make it three nights in a row and prove that she was falling in love with him. "He's obviously not so boring after all, by the looks of things," I said.

And OK, I might not have worded it perfectly but I certainly didn't deserve her reply: "Mind your own bloody business!"

Grr.

Monday 7 July – 6.00 a.m.

Here comes Malibu sneaking in again. It's like Groundhog flaming Day!

7.35 a.m.

Bet Malibu's still asleep. Actually, now's the perfect time to wake her – get her to admit that she's fallen for Boring Roger and put a stop to this bull. (Much easier to get the truth out of a dozy head.) Still won't come straight out and ask her, though. I'm going to play the fool. Reel her in. Ask silly, random questions until she feels so in control, she accidentally slips up.

Basically, methinks I'm going to get Columbo on Malibu's ass.

7.40 a.m.

OMG. That girl is so—ooo bloody rude!

If she doesn't want to share a tiny bit of info with her own sister, she can rot in bed for all I care.

8.29 a.m.

Malibu's running late (surprise, surprise) so I'm leaving for work without her. She doesn't deserve me to wait for her anyway, after the names she just called me.

Oh well, the day can only get better from here. Actually expecting to have a good one because I'm sure the Feminazi is going to big me up for the new colour-coded booking system. ☺

7 p.m.

That's IT. Don't think I can stand another second in the same room as the Feminazi!

Today she lectured me about changing the booking system without checking with her first. So I defended myself by saying I just wanted to improve it. Then she pointed outside and said, "Tell me what the sign says on that door."

"Kara's," I muttered.

"That's right – Kara's, not REMY'S," she replied. What a cow!

I've had enough. I'm going to search online for a new job.

10 P.M.

Oops! Job-hunting didn't quite happen. Robbie phoned and we had luv chatter for over an hour. Well, I say luv chatter but a lot of our conversation was about football (which I know absolutely nothing about). His training went well – he's set himself a target of scoring twenty goals this season (he's a striker).

"Oh, like Frank Lampard," I said, totally winging it.

"No, not really," he answered. "Frank Lampard plays central midfield."

"Doh! Yeah, of course he does." *WTF is central midfield?*

I told him I'd had a crap day at work. And when I repeated what Kara had said, he came out with, "Don't worry about it – it's typical girls' stuff, innit. You'll all be best friends by tomorrow."

"Hmm." I sighed, not convinced.

"Anyway, whatcha doing Thursday?" he asked, and he turned my day around by inviting me out on a double date with his best friend on the team! His name's Terry Dawson and his girlfriend is called Paris.

James phoned straight after, and when I told him about the double date he confirmed what I was thinking: "That's definitely a girlfriend-boyfriend thing to do. He must be taking you seriously." Yippee!

Then he announced that he'd passed his hairdressing NVQ!

After I congratulated him, we had a right bitch about the Feminazi. And I decided that as I'd probably find out about my NVQ tomorrow, it'd be best to look for a new job then.

So it's all good. ☺

10.30 P.M.

I never thought I'd be saying this, but I'm worried about Malibu. She's just been arguing with someone on the phone. Shouting. Name-calling. Swearing. The whole lot. So I went into her room when she'd hung up and asked if she was all right.

"What the hell do you think?" she screamed at me.

"Ugh! What's wrong with you? You're like a bloody schizo at the minute!"

"Have you finished?"

"No I bloody well haven't," I replied. "I want my sister back. On a full-time basis. Not every now and then, like it's been lately!"

I waited for her to shout something back at me, but her face crumpled and then she started to cry. I rushed over to hug her but her whole body tensed up and she shrieked, "Don't touch me! Just go!"

So I did.

I don't know what's happened, but I reckon Boring Roger has got something to do with it.

Tuesday 8 July – 8 a.m.

Malibu's been crying all night. She wouldn't talk to Mum, Dad or even me about it. She said she just wanted to be left alone. How can Boring Roger go from being her fail-safe to reducing her to this?

Anyway, I have to tell the Feminazi she's not coming to work today.

1 p.m.

I've come home for lunch because I wanted to check up on Malibu. Not that she's saying much. She won't eat a thing, either, and her eyes are red-raw. I told her, "Forget him, Malibu, he isn't even on your level. He's nothing compared with Lance." But that just made her cry again. ☹

It's made me realize that things aren't that bad for me at the moment – Robbie's been great. My only problem is work. I'm definitely going to jack in Kara's as soon as I get my NVQ.

I rushed into work today expecting my NVQ to be handed over, but I got nada. So I had to bite my tongue every time the Feminazi ordered me to do something. The only thing that kept me going was imagining where I'd stick that NVQ as soon as I got it.

<u>7 P.M.</u>

James just called and asked me to join him for an NVQ celebration drink at the pub. I told him that I'd like to come (even though I haven't got mine yet) but I wasn't sure about leaving Malibu.

"She can come too, if she likes," he said.

"OK, I'll invite her – but don't hold your breath."

If Malibu would prefer me to stay in with her, I'll do that instead – after all, she stayed in and watched *Titanic* with me when I was going mental about Robbie. It's the least I can do.

<u>7.15 P.M.</u>

Malibu didn't want to come, but she told me to go without her. I feel a bit bad because she looked miserable.

"Are you sure you don't want to talk?" I asked.

"There's nothing to talk about," she replied. "It's over." ☹

<u>7.25 P.M.</u>

Robbie just called and I'm sure I detected jealousy when I said I was going out with James.

"Who's this James fella then?"

"Oh, just a friend."

"With benefits?" he asked.

I laughed and said, "No. A friend with absolutely no benefits. Not now. Not before. And not ever, ever, ever. You have nothing to worry about, believe me."

But I didn't explain why because I quite liked leaving him to stew a little bit. It's only what I had to do when he was away.

7.45 p.m.

OK. I'm dressed and ready to hit the pub. It took ages because James is really critical about clothes, hair, make-up and all that. With most boys you know you can throw on a short skirt or a tight top and they'll be happy just perving, but that doesn't work with James – fashion is his number-one priority.

I decided to wear my harem pants (so–oo now) with a black vest.

7.50 p.m.

Nearly forgot my fake ID. Phew!

11 p.m.

Well, I can honestly say that I made a proper idiot of myself tonight.

I was just getting into the celebrations when Boring Roger walked into the pub. With a girl on his arm. The red mist came tumbling down. I stormed up to him and threw my drink in his face.

"You tosser!" I said. "You absolute—" (I can't remember the details but I know I called him every swear word I could think of.)

The girl he was with started to scream and cry, James tried to calm me down and Roger kept shouting things like "You're mad!" and "What the hell are you on about?"

"You know exactly what I'm on about!" I shouted back, launching myself at him. And I might even have hit him if James hadn't grabbed me around the waist and dragged me back.

"Look, mate," Roger said to James. "You'd better keep that nutter away from me, because I might not be responsible for what happens next."

"What? You gonna hit me? You that weak and pathetic?" I shrieked at him.

Then he looked me in the eye and said quietly through clenched teeth, "I'd never hit a woman. I think you know what kind of person I am."

"What? Like I knew that you wouldn't dump my sister? She's at home crying her eyes out because of you!" I yelled.

"What you on about? No one has shed more tears about your sister than me," he said. "And let me tell you, she hasn't returned any of my calls in about two weeks. So

129

if she's crying, it has nothing to do with me – and everything to do with someone else."

I wanted to call him a liar, but his eyes looked like he was telling the truth. I was so–oo confused. Still didn't apologize when he asked me to, though (just in case). Then he walked off with his date.

I convinced myself I'd done the right thing when James put me into a cab, and even on the way home. Then I received a text from Kellie: *OMG. Have you heard?? Lance and Amy Fitzgerald are getting married!! WTF?!*

Now suddenly everything makes sense. And I feel like a right twot.

<u>11.30 P.M.</u>

Everything happens for a reason. If Boring Roger hadn't walked into the pub tonight, Malibu would probably still be keeping all her pain about Lance Wilson to herself. She looked bloody relieved after I got her to confess.

"I love him, Rem," she said. "I've always loved him. When he rang me up a couple of weeks ago and gave me a long speech about wanting me back, I said no way because I know what a player he is. Then you saw him kissing Amy and I got jealous, so I called him, ranting and raving. He told me *I* was the one he wanted to be with, so I fell for it and went over to his house."

"But you said you were going to Roger's that night!"

"I know. I was just embarrassed about telling you to be

130

strong and then being weak myself. I was going to tell you, I swear. I would've had to, with the way things were going, but then … he changed his mind again and…"

She stopped. *Is she going to cry?* I thought. And just when I was convinced that Malibu had become a soft-hearted Disney princess, she said, "I mean – dissed for a dog like Amy Fitzgerald? What a fucking cheek!" ☺

Wednesday 9 July – 7 P.M.

Malibu looked a bit down first thing, but as soon as she got to work she switched on her personality. Ding!

Goldenballs called her at about eleven, and after that it was Gary, Gary, Gary for the rest of the day (as if Lance and heartbreak had never existed). It must have been fake but it was bloody convincing.

I'm pretty fed up myself. Still haven't heard about my NVQ. At lunchtime I asked the Feminazi if she knew what was going on and she said, "Ask the Royal Mail. I'm not a postman."

7.30 P.M.

Bloody Nosy Knickers Nicole Walker just phoned me.

"Is it true that Lance Wilson is marrying Amy Fitzgerald?"

"Yeah… Think so," I replied.

"How's Malibu taking it?" she asked, dying to be filled in. "She must be gutted."

"Can we speak later, please, Nicole?" I said. "I'm look-ing for a job."

"A job? Why, what's happened at Kara's?"

"Nothing. Speak soon, OK?" I answered, and put the phone down. Wish I hadn't said anything – don't need her spreading the news before I find somewhere else to work.

8 P.M.

The only job I can find in the area is one where I'd have to rent a space from the salon owner, and then the money I make will be mine. But you need to have a good customer base before you do something like that. I haven't even got started. So–oo annoying!

8.03 P.M.

Mum called me for dinner for the thousandth time, but I told her I wasn't hungry. Going to stay in my room and wal-low in my work depression. ☹

8.30 P.M.

James always says that by the time he was ten, he was sure of two things: 1. He was never, ever going to fancy a girl, and 2. He wanted to be a hairdresser.

It wasn't until I was thirteen, when Malibu would come back from work buzzing and then use me as her manicure/pedicure guinea pig (that's all Mum would allow her to try on me), that I decided I wanted to be a beautician too. But at ten there's one thing I was sure of: whatever I chose to do, I needed to be in charge.

I hated being bossed about by Malibu only to turn up at school and be bossed about by all the teachers as well (except Mrs Stevens – loved her English lessons). I hated all the petty rules about wearing the correct uniform and not running in the corridors (even if you were dying to go to the loo and the corridor was empty apart from you and the teacher who just happened to spot you – duh!). I couldn't wait to grow up so I could do things MY way. And not just for the sake of it: I felt sure there was a better way to do most things – and that I could find that better way if I put my mind to it.

That colour-coded system I devised the other day was bloody genius and the only reason it wasn't appreciated was because it's not my salon. Well, you know what? Maybe I do need to be in charge and it's time to get my own salon RIGHT NOW.

8.31 p.m.

Yeah, right. I can't even understand basic business terms, how the hell am I going to run my own salon?

Can't see me having one until I'm old and miserable like the Feminazi. ☹

Dad came into my room, worried about me not eating dinner. I told him I had no intention of fainting again any time soon.

"Good. Well, what's the matter then?"

"Nothing," I grumbled.

"Of course there bloody well is – look at the face on you! What is it?"

I sighed. "I think I've got a problem with authority."

Dad laughed. "Don't be daft," he said. "Is it Kara again?"

I nodded and told him I blooming well hate my job, giving him the prime opportunity to start on about how I should have stayed on at school. But he didn't. Instead he said, "Remy, I've seen the attention you put into doing your friends' nails when they come over here. You love making people look good."

"Yeah, but I don't want to be doing it for the rest of my life," I told him.

Dad looked confused. "Please don't tell me you left school for nothing," he said – just as I expected. Only he didn't sound angry – I could have handled that. It was the disappointment in his voice that I couldn't stand. "Please don't tell me," he continued, "that I listened as you stood right there, on that very spot, and told me you wanted to be a beautician – and that I was stupid enough to believe you."

"You weren't stupid," I answered. "And it isn't as simple as that."

"Yes, it is. Now, do you want to be a beautician or don't you?" he asked.

"Yes… No. Yes. No. Yes… Sort of."

"Sort of? What the hell does 'sort of' mean?"

"It means … I want to have my OWN salon," I said. And it felt good to actually say it out loud. Then it stopped just being a dream and became real.

"Really?" Dad suddenly sounded happier. "Remy, that's great! And you could do it, too."

"Not yet. Probably when I'm older."

"Of course you can do it now! Deborah Gordon started her first business at sixteen. It's just whether you're willing to put the work in."

His faith in me made me smile, so I told him I'd even started making a business plan. He offered to take a look at it, because running his own business with Uncle Pete means he knows a thing or two. I explained that it was still at an early stage (no point letting him know that I'd abandoned it to update my Facebook page) and that I'd show it to him when I was happier with it.

"OK," he said. "Well, at least let me know the start-up cost."

"Huh? Um… I'm still fine-tuning that, too," I bluffed.

"Great. Well, I'm really proud of you, Remy." And he looked it. In fact he looked so proud, I finally realized how gutted he must have felt about me ditching A levels.

I feel proud of myself too and I haven't even done anything yet!

So I'm going to spend the rest of the night on my business plan. Will begin by typing "What is a start-up cost?" into Google. ☺

Thursday 10 July – Double-Date Day!!!
9 a.m.

I've just woken up. Good job it's my day off. Stayed up God knows how late last night working out my salon start-up cost – which is basically how much I'll have to spend up front to be able to open a staffed, furnished and fully equipped salon. Nightmare. It took three hours! (And I'm crap at maths, so three earth hours felt more like six to me.) All to finally work out that I'll need about forty grand! Where on earth am I going to get forty grand from? Nowhere, that's where. I have about £200 in the bank and if I keep saving at the rate I do, I won't be able to open a salon until I'm five hundred and twenty-two! (And I don't need to be Carol Vorderman to calculate that.)

Grr.

It's depressing, but I'm going to have to knuckle down and keep on working at Kara's until I win the lottery or something. (Yeah, right.)

9.30 a.m.

OMG. I've got great big bags under my eyes. I'm going to look awful for DD (double date). Will have to paint on the concealer, because I bet any money that Terry's girlfriend, Paris, is going to be some glamour model that puts me to shame. Methinks this mission is going to call for some chicken fillets! And on second thoughts, concrete instead of concealer. ☹

Brainwave! I once read in *Grazia* that on the day of a photoshoot some models brew two teabags, lie down and then stick them under their eyes to get rid of dark circles. Will try it. ☺

9.50 a.m.

Grrr… My "de-bagging" session was interrupted by the Feminazi. She called and asked if I could pop into the salon if I wasn't too busy. I wanted to say, "Of course I'm too bloody busy, I've got eyes to de-bag, a DD outfit to sort out and a Facebook page to update."

But I need Kara just now so I said OK.

2 p.m.

Today is the best day ever for three reasons:

1. I passed my NVQ!

2. When Kara presented me with my certificate she said, "And I've decided to continue with your colour-coded booking system." She even said I could take her colour – green – as she doesn't need to do treatments now that I'm qualified.

How could something that simple make me feel like I'd got through the first round of *X Factor*? Because it did. And all I could do on the way home was daydream about what my own salon would look like (if I lived in a parallel universe and had forty grand in the bank instead of £223.07).

3. I'm only hours away from my double date with Robbie, Terry and Paris, and I just know it's going to be fantastico!!

7 P.M.

Right, I've laid out my DD outfit and am now about to jump into the shower. After much toing and froing I've decided to go with the maxi dress because if Paris is a skinny-model type, my bum will look even more massive in a tight-fitting dress or jeans – but if she's got big bazookas, I can at least pretend that I have a decent pair with my chest-enhancing fillets. I just hope I don't fall asleep at the table … I still feel bloody knackered.

Midnight

I'm home! Thank God. The restaurant was beautiful. Hakkasan, it was called. It's so–oo lush. By far the poshest Chinese restaurant I've ever been to. And it would have been a perfect night if it hadn't been for Paris. She's an absolute mentalist! Her lips have been moulded into a pout, her fake tan makes her look like she's bathed in three cans of Tango, her legs reach up to her armpits, the dress she was wearing looked more like a top than a dress, and there is no way she ever thinks before she opens her mouth.

When we were introduced, I shook her hand and said, "What a lovely dress."

"Versace," she replied. "Twelve hundred quid."

When I told the three of them how happy I was about passing my NVQ, Paris turned to Robbie and said, "You ain't gonna let your bird wax people's backsides, are ya?" Robbie went bright red.

She even followed me to the Ladies, saying that she wanted to powder her nose (if she'd put on any more, she'd have looked like a clown – a burnt-orange one). Then she turned to me as soon as we got inside and said, "Remy, a little word of advice. You're pretty. You've got a good pair of boobs. So never, ever go out with a footballer and then dress yourself in a tent."

A tent?!

"Your dress is great," Robbie said when I asked him what he thought about it on the way home. "Could have been a bit…" He stopped.

"A bit what?"

"A bit more sexy then. All right? But it's nice."

"Sexy?" I repeated. "Sexy how? Sexy like Paris?" I spat out her bloody name.

"God, no. Nothing like Paris. She's not a proper girl."

"No?" I said, slightly relieved. "What is she then?"

"You're too innocent for this stuff, princess," he replied.

"Is she a prostitute?" I exclaimed, thinking I'd just had my first encounter with a real-life prostitute and she was nothing like the ones on *The Bill*.

"Nah." He laughed. "At least a prostitute gets paid."

I frowned. "What? I don't get it."

"OK," he said, as if he was Dad giving in to my pleas to be told the facts of life. "Girls like Paris target guys like us – so they end up getting used and abused."

"Yeah, right, by having loads of money thrown at them for Versace dresses?" I scoffed.

"That's nothing to Terry, princess. He makes that kind of money sitting on the toilet. But when he wants to get serious, she'll get binned and he'll find himself a proper girl."

"Oh. Right." It hadn't occurred to me that footballers actually knew they were being targeted by WAG wannabes. I suppose that's why Malibu invented the Charter – a way to make it look like she couldn't care less about pulling one. (When it's actually all she's been thinking about for the past five years.)

"So … what am I to you then?" I asked.

We'd just pulled up outside my house. Robbie turned to me, gently touched my face and said, "You're the real thing, princess. Wife material."

And then he kissed me and kissed me and kiss–sssssssed me!

Had a crappy night's sleep. Can't help thinking that Robbie will go elsewhere if I hold out for another five and a half weeks, like Malibu says I should. It's not like he'll be short of offers. Nearly SIX WEEKS? That's a blooming lifetime!! Besides, I'm not sure I need to keep it up. If he thinks I'm wife material, that means the WAG Charter has already worked. Job done.

What2do? What2do?

7.30 p.m.

Wow! Just finished making Mum up, and it was HER who asked ME to do it. Almost had a heart attack.

"What's brought this on?" I asked.

"Nothing special," she said, but her eyes twinkled, so I figured she wanted to please Dad. ☺

First, I applied a grey eye shadow to make her blue eyes stand out, then a bit of silver in the arch of her eyebrow, black mascara, bronzing to the cheekbones and a touch of melon-pink lip gloss, and I can honestly say that once I'd finished she looked a million bucks. Just like the old days.

"Thank you, Remy," she said, gazing into the mirror.

"Pleasure," I replied.

And it truly was a pleasure to transform some-one's appearance, seeing as I spent most of my time on reception today (even though I'm now a proper beauty

141

therapist). Grr. It's gutting because I get commission for doing treat-ments, and I could really do with the extra money. It'll help pay for all the clothes I have to buy for my dates with Robbie. ☺

In our lunch break I managed to have a word with Malibu about the WAG Charter.

"Do I really, really need to hold out for eight weeks?" I asked after telling her what Robbie had said when he dropped me home.

"I dunno why you want my advice after the mess I've made of things, but in my opinion…" She thought about it for a second and then said, "Don't play games. Just do what you feel."

Yay!

Then I checked that she was all right, because today all the gossip in the salon seemed to be about Lance and Amy getting married. No one could believe it. And when Malibu's client – Lorraine the Pain – asked her how she felt about it, Malibu said, "I don't give a flying fuck." But I, of course, knew she did.

"Don't you worry about me," she said. "I'm going to Gary's tomorrow night."

"Really?"

"Yep. The new Posh and Becks mission is back on! Only bigger and better this time. Which is probably why I said you can forget about holding out, because I certainly don't intend to." She wiggled her eyebrows up and down, then broke into a cheeky grin.

"You minx," I said. But it was good to see her actually having a laugh.

<u>10 P.M.</u>

Malibu watched a DVD in her room while I watched *The Entrepreneur* with Mum and Dad. Very surprising episode tonight – the favourite went out. He's v. posh and called Tristan. "I went to Oxford, you know" was his favourite line. Dad always said, "So bloody what," but everyone else on the program seemed to worship the ground he walked on. This was the first time he'd been hauled in front of Deborah Gordon, and when she pointed at him and said, "You're outta here," Dad clapped and said, "Couldn't have happened to a nicer bloke. Obnoxious pillock."

When it was over, Mum went to make a cup of tea and Dad asked me how the business plan was coming along. I felt bad telling him I'd given up, but I couldn't see a way round it.

"Not great. The start-up cost comes to about forty grand!"

"Forty grand?" he repeated. "That's toppy for a bit of nail varnish."

"It's not just nail varnish, you know! There's the cost of nail bars, fake tan, wax, facial creams, a laser skin-rejuvenation machine – and they're dead expensive."

"What do you need a laser thingamajig for then?"

"Because…" I was going to say "because Kara has one",

but then I realized this wasn't Kara's we were talking about. This was MY salon. And I could do anything I wanted.

"It sounds to me like you're starting too big," Dad said. "Think of just doing the basics for now, and then you've got room to expand."

I realized he was right.

"And then of course you'll need less of a loan," he said, as if it was obvious.

"A loan?"

"Well, that's what the business plan is for, isn't it? Or have you come into some money that I don't know about?" He laughed at his own joke.

"Um… No, of course not," I said, laughing back. (Thinking: *A loan!*)

"Right. Less money borrowed means you can pay back earlier. Just make sure you forecast your profits clearly – and realistically, of course."

"Of course," I agreed, nodding seriously as if I knew what he was talking about.

"Show that you'll be able to pay off the loan in about three to five years and Bob's your auntie's husband."

He made it sound so–oo simple, but I know it's going to be hard work. The difference is that now I know I can get a loan, I'm not going to give up. ☺

10.30 P.M.

Yay! I've been doing some research for my salon. There's

144

big money in spray-tan booths. Apparently they're going to get more and more popular because everyone wants to be brown, but the government are pushing the fact that sunbeds are lethal… Cue the spray tan!

The Feminazi pays us to spray customers, but there are automatic booths that can do it instead. The best one is called Tanarama and it delivers a spray tan in just six minutes! It's so—oo expensive, though. £15,000! I thought no bloody way am I spending that on one piece of equipment – until I read on the Tanarama website that if you charge £25 per treatment and get fifty customers a week, you'll make £50,000 a year.

Fifty grand! And you don't even have to pay a beautician.

I'm going to take Dad's advice and cut back on the other things I wanted to buy – a laser skin-rejuvenation machine, for a start.

<u>10.45 P.M.</u>

I've cracked the budget problem! My salon is going to specialize in three things: nails, tans and waxes. That way I'll only need a couple of beauticians, because the tanning booth will be like having another two pairs of hands!

Genius.

Now I'm going to look online for a sample business plan so I can learn how to forecast profits. And I'll make sure I type in *basic business plan* this time, so I don't get confused.

Go "quantify" that! ☺

11 P.M.

OMG. Went online and realized I hadn't checked my emails today. Godfather Alan had sent this:

Hey Remy,

I hope you're well. I've decided to come back sooner rather than later. Hopefully I'll be there on Sunday.

See you then,

Alan x

Sunday?! That's like two days away. This is definitely the best week ever!!!!!!

Saturday 12 July – 7.40 a.m.

Last night I dreamt about what my salon will look like. I can't believe it! I'm dating a hot Premiership footballer yet I'm dreaming about Tanarama spray-tan booths and Essie nail colours. Doh!

In my dream, everything was absolutely purrfect. My salon had white side walls and a bright-pink back wall that had a framed sign hanging on it that said: *Get your wax done. Get your tan done. Get your nails done. Ta-dah!* Hanging from the ceiling was a hu–uuge glitterball that didn't stop shimmering. But the best bit was that the queue to get in ran out into the street. I wish. ☺

I just called Robbie, because when he phoned last night I was talking like a zombie. (Was right in the middle of looking at business-plan samples.)

"Sorry about last night, babe, I was really stressed out," I said.

"What're you stressing about?"

"My business plan."

"Your business plan for what?" he asked.

"My OWN salon," I said, making him the second person in the world I've ever told.

I waited for him to be impressed, but he just went, "Oh … right."

He probably still had the hump with me because I really was useless over the phone last night ("uh-huh, hmm, yeah" is basically all I said). So I added quickly, "Anyway, I promise to make it up to you."

And that perked him up. "Oh yeah? How're you gonna do that?"

I put on a German accent and said, "I have vays."

He started to chuckle and everything was all right again. "Well, I'm looking forward to it, princess," he told me. "Let's meet up tomorrow, about seven-thirty. I can't go out tonight – I've got a pre-season match tomorrow afternoon."

"Dealio," I replied.

"D'you want me to pick you up from yours this time?"

I thought about it. Wouldn't it be great for Mum to see that I WAS pretty enough to pull a footballer? Surely that would be worth Dad giving him the threatening eyes.

"Great," I said. "I'll text you the address. Better go to work now, baby."

"OK. I'll bell you later."

Then the rest of the conversation went like this:

"Bye, babe."

"Bye, princess…"

"You end the call."

"No, you end the call."

"No–ooo, you," I said.

Then he did.

7 P.M.

Yay! Did two treatments today on people who had just walked in. One simple chin and upper lip wax on a girl who hated the pain so much, she gulped loudly every time I tore away a wax strip. And a pedicure for a lady who had the smelliest feet ever! She was wearing trainers with no socks on, and when she took them off we should have fumigated the whole place. Mouldy Gorgonzola. Yuck!

But apart from that, I had a right laugh. Especially when Blow-dry Sarah came back from the coffee run clutching a copy of *Now* magazine, waving it about as if it was the last golden ticket to Willy Wonka's chocolate factory.

"Check this out!" she said, slamming the magazine down on the reception desk. Natasha was free, so she came over to see what the fuss was about. The Feminazi was off collecting clean towels and Malibu was at her nail station, mid-manicure but peering across at us.

Blow-dry Sarah rifled through the mag until she got to the "Spotted" page, then pointed to a picture of Sarah Harding coming out of the Orchid Bar.

"She looks great," I said, wondering what the drama was about.

"Do you think so?" said Natasha. "I'm not sure. She—"

"Not THAT," Blow-dry Sarah cut in. "THIS!"

She put her finger right on the edge of the picture, and there, way behind Sarah Harding, was an out-of-focus blonde figure in a neon-orange dress. You couldn't make out the face because it was literally a dot, but it had to be Malibu!

"Look, Mal, you've made it!" said Blow-dry, running to Malibu's nail station to show her the photo.

"So I have," said Malibu icily.

She was silent for the rest of the day. Until we got out of the salon, that is.

"Do you know how bloody embarrassing that was?" she screeched as soon as our feet hit the pavement. "What's the point of being in a magazine if no one can even tell it's YOU?"

I decided the safest response was to just shrug.

"And why was Blow-dry showing it to everyone who came through the door?" she exploded. "It's like she didn't realize that nobody could bloody make me out except for HER. I could have been Osama Bin Laden for all anyone else knew!"

"Maybe the other pictures they took will turn up," I said to make her feel better.

"What other pictures?"

"Dunno. I thought you said had some taken with Golden— I mean, Gary."

"I didn't have any taken with Gary."

I frowned, confused. "Huh? I thought you said you had your picture taken."

"*I* did. But Gary hates paparazzi, so he went out the back way. I stepped out the front, saw the flashbulbs going off and… God, they could have at least got me in focus!"

It dawned on me that that picture really was the only record of Malibu's big moment.

"Was that IT?" I exclaimed.

She just glared at me. So I shut up.

Well, Posh and Becks can sleep soundly tonight.

8 P.M.

As planned, Malibu's gone to Gary's house. The big surprise of the night is that Mum has asked me to teach her to blow-dry her hair salon-style. She is so–ooo coming out of complacency mode. ☺

<u>11.30 P.M.</u>

Popped out for a few drinks with Kel. Not sure Mum and Dad heard me come back in, because they're not even hissing – they're arguing at the tops of their voices.

"You're a liar!" Dad's just shouted. "A bloody liar. Just like I thought!"

So glad Godfather Alan's coming tomorrow. Planning to hand the mediator role straight back over to him. And now I don't have that responsibility, I'm putting on my headphones and turning Rihanna up to ten.

<u>Sunday 13 July – 10 a.m.</u>

I love Sundays when Mum's in a good mood, because when she's happy she makes us a full-on breakfast. I woke up to the smell of eggs and bacon, so I thought she and Dad must have kissed and made up. But then I walked past the living room and noticed that Dad was there, folding up a blanket on the sofa. ☹

"Cheers, Mum," I said, going into the kitchen and rubbing crust out of my eyes.

"Pleasure," she said, all chirpy.

"Where's Malibu?"

"She stayed out last night. I'm quite glad about it after all those tears we've had." She frowned at me. "What's so funny?"

"Nothing," I said, thinking: *Malibu and GOLDEN-*

BALLS! OMG – it's only been three weeks!!

Then Dad walked in and made his way to the kettle, and they both did that thing again where they twist their shoulders to avoid touching each other.

"Good morning, Dad," I said.

"Is it?" he grumbled. He looked absolutely miserable.

I couldn't believe it. It was like Freaky Friday, only it was Sunday – and instead of me swapping personalities with Mum, DAD and Mum had done it instead. I nearly told the pair of them to sort themselves out, but then I remembered that's Alan's job now, so I left it.

7 P.M.

Dad's been AWOL since eleven o'clock this morning. He made a proper show of leaving, too, by slamming the front door with an almighty thud. I decided that worrying about it wouldn't achieve anything, so I spent my day dreaming about having my own salon instead. It's become an obsession. And it's definitely the thing I want more than anything else in the world right now. Along with Robbie, of course.

Kellie popped in at lunchtime and we had a right laugh about the double date and Paris's "don't dress in a tent" advice.

"When you told me a maxi dress hides a multitude of sins, I didn't think you meant it bloody smothered them," I joked.

"Paris sounds like a hot mess." Kellie laughed.

Then I must have drifted off into my salon daydream for a moment, because she frowned and said, "What're you thinking about?"

So I told her how badly I want to have my own salon and about the business plan and the loan. And she said she was really proud of me and would support me however she could. She even gave me her cousin Rachel's email address because she's just started her own business too. I was going to email her after Kellie left but I've been trying to find the right (non-tent) sexy outfit to wear.

7.10 P.M.

OMG. Robbie will be here in twenty minutes and I still have no idea what to wear!

7.20 P.M.

I phoned James.

"He–eeeelp! I need to look hot in fifteen minutes!"

"I'm probably a bit too high fashion for a footballer's taste," he told me. So I ran through all my options: the tight blue jeans with the satin silver top, the gold sequined dress that stops at my knees, or the red boy-magnet dress I nicked from Malibu's wardrobe when she went to the pub (about two minutes ago).

"I like the idea of the red dress," James said. "Will it fit you?"

"It's Lycra," I said. "It'll stretch."

"Go for it."

So I have. And it doesn't look too bad. (Even if I say so myself.)

<u>7.25 P.M.</u>

Can't believe it – Mum has done her hair and make-up and it looks almost as good as when I did it! That will certainly get Dad's attention (when he finally decides to come home). It's been eight and half hours since he stropped out. Must be turning into a diva in his old age!

<u>7.27 P.M.</u>

Robbie just texted to say he's three minutes away. Perfecto.

That's funny. Mum's just opened the front door, but it can't be Robbie and I didn't hear the doorbell.

I can hear Dad shouting! When did *he* get back?

And now Mum's shouting too!

<u>8 P.M.</u>

Can't stop crying. Feel like my whole world's turned upside down.

"Go on, tell her!" Dad yelled at Mum when I came to the front door to see what was going on. He was clearly drunk. OK, so he's been known to have a few pints, but this was different. Tonight he was drunk to the power of nine!

"Tell me what?" I asked, confused.

"Reg, you're drunk. Stop being so childish!" Mum sounded panicky.

"Tell her!" he shouted again. He was swaying all over the place. "Or I will."

"Tell me WHAT?" I repeated, noticing that the nosy neighbours from across the road were sweeping their curtains back to get a good look.

"Your mum's been having an affair."

I frowned, thinking he must have got it wrong. Mum just isn't the type.

"Reg, please. No!"

He pointed at her, still swaying, and said, "Too late now. This is your bloody fault. You're the one who told him to come back!"

"I didn't. I swear to you," she said. "I just thanked him for sending Remy that money."

"And he suddenly jumps on a plane from Australia?" he screamed. "Do you think I'm stupid?!"

I clicked that they were talking about Godfather Alan.

"Dad, please," I intervened. "If you're talking about Alan, he's been wanting to come back for ages. He didn't say he was coming because he wanted to surprise you. That's all."

"Who told you that?" Dad demanded.

"Alan did. If I knew it was going to cause a problem, I'd have—"

Dad interrupted to bellow at Mum, "Getting Remy involved in your sordid little affair? Do you have no shame?"

"Alan would never do something like that!" Mum snapped. And she sounded so defensive, so heartfelt, that it made me nervous.

"Mum?" I asked. "What's going on?"

There was a slight pause – a two-second window that helped me to prepare, allowed me to see the guilt on her face.

"I'm sorry, Remy," she mumbled. My heart dropped.

"You'll be sorry, all right," Dad sneered. "And you can jump straight on that plane and piss off back to Australia with him, because Remy's still MY daughter!"

"It's not as simple as that," Mum protested.

"Yes it is. We made a deal. And she's not eighteen yet."

Deal? Eighteen? I thought. *WTF?*

"But she's only a few months off," Mum argued. "She might as well do it now."

"Do what now?" I demanded, starting to panic.

As I said that, a black Range Rover pulled up across the road. Robbie. How embarrassing – we must have looked like a family on *The Jeremy Kyle Show*. Bad enough for him to realize that it was not the time to get out of his car, anyway. Now I wish I'd run to his car and driven off with him. But I had to know the truth.

"Well?" I persisted. Mum and Dad were now dead silent, looking at each other awkwardly. "Do. What. Now?"

Dad's eyes dropped to the pavement. Mum couldn't

look at me either – her eyes went everywhere except to my face.

"A test," she said reluctantly.

"A test FOR…?"

Then Mum's face softened. Became the most loving I'd ever seen it. She walked up to me and gently put her hands on my shoulders.

"Listen, Rem," she said. "We're not sure, but…"

"Alan thinks he could be your real dad," Dad blurted out.

Just like that. My whole world crushed with a few little words.

scan the code to watch a video
of Michelle Gayle reading from this book:

Friday 17 October – 10 a.m.

Haven't felt like writing for ages. But today I finally got the urge. I think it's because I've settled into my new routine. Well, almost – some things still need getting used to. Still find it hard to believe that I live here, for a start. Sometimes I have to pinch myself. Actually, I almost did when Robbie told me he didn't want me to leave.

"I know I said you should stay for a few days, till you sorted your head out about your parents," he said, "but I know I want to be with you. So what's the point in you looking for a flat?"

There was no way I was going to live under the same roof as Mum. Not after she'd said she wanted to be with Alan. So I'd been searching for accommodation in my local papers and, I admit, cringing at what I could afford to rent on my crappy wages. Still, I had my pride. "That way there's no pressure on you," I told Robbie. "I don't want you to feel like you HAVE to put me up."

He ran his finger along my eyebrows and said, "That's exactly why I like you, princess. You don't expect anything. But trust me, I WANT you to stay. Because I'm crazy about you." Then he kissed me. Not any old kiss. This was an MTV Movie Award-winning kiss. And no one – not Leonardo, nor Robert Pattinson – could have kissed me better. Then he took my hand and led me to the bedroom. That's the first time we went all the way. It was perfect. His body, his touch, his EVERYTHING, and I've been here ever since.

Sometimes I think, *Wow!* I used to sit at home dreaming about moving out of the box bedroom at Mum and Dad's, and look at me now – four bedrooms, four bathrooms and a massive garden with a pool, in a private road in the posh part of Essex. And all thanks to Robbie.

Even though it's been three months now, I'm still careful about not breaking cups and plates, as if I'm in someone else's house. And I suppose technically it *is* Robbie's house – but he likes to say that it's ours.

"Look at me now." That's what Deborah Gordon says at the start of *The Entrepreneur*, just before they show her huge glass building. Except she earned that building, and I suppose the only thing that makes me feel uncomfortable is knowing that I didn't really earn this house – not through working, anyway. Although I am starting to realize that what the other wives and girlfriends (I hate saying WAGs now) tell me is true – I'll earn it in other ways.

My new routine felt weird at first, but Robbie was right when he said I should give up work. Doing that two-hour journey to and from Kara's, then the washing and cooking once I'd got home, only made me knackered all the time. What's the point in that? Besides, it was the least I could do for him after all he'd done for me. Now he actually has a girlfriend who's around when he finishes training so we can go for lunch or out shopping (if he doesn't play golf with his team mates). And I'm not knackered any more, so I can concentrate on keeping the house how he likes it and learning how to cook as well as his mum. It was obviously the right thing to do, so I can't work out why I miss Kara's so much – the girls, the banter, even the Feminazi herself sometimes. Doh! I must need my head checked. Or probably just a little more time to adjust.

James and Kellie seem to need double, triple adjusting time. If I hear either of them say "You've changed" one more time, I think I'll scream. James hardly phones and has said that he can't make it every time I've invited him to watch Robbie play. And just when I finally have a credit card and the budget to buy whatever designer thing I like, Kellie never wants to come shopping with me.

"I haven't got any money," she said the last time I was going to Selfridges. So I offered to buy her something and she replied that she'd rather pay her own way in life – which was a definite dig.

Malibu says I should drop her because she's jealous. But Malibu's all right. She loves living with Gary in Surrey and has really thrown herself into the Chelsea WAG set. (I know I just said the "w" word but it saves so much time.) Surrey is bloody miles away, so I feel like I've lost Malibu as well – and I don't fit in that well with the girls here. I'm trying v. hard, but Essex is like a separate country, with its own way to dress and behave and talk. So I'm really looking forward to seeing Malibu today. We're taking Dad to lunch. Yay! I haven't seen him for two whole weeks!

10.30 a.m.

Dad just called. He said Malibu had told him to prepare for a surprise and he wanted to know if I knew what it was. (He hates surprises.) I joked that Gary's probably bought her a jumbo jet (thinking, *To go with the Rolex watch, Cartier bracelet and Chanel handbag*).

"Essex hasn't stolen your sense of humour then," Dad joked back.

"Nope. Still alive and kicking," I replied.

He said he was going to look at a flat before he came for lunch. (Methinks three months on Uncle Pete's sofa has done his head in.)

"Bye…" I said. "Love you."

"Love you too," he said before ringing off.

Before, I would rather have walked barefoot on burning

hot coals than say anything so Disney – but I try to end all my calls to Dad like that now. I want him to know how much I appreciate him, because I learnt a lot when I was waiting for the results of that bloody DNA test: mostly that Dad is a full-blown saint. He has to be, to have forgiven Mum for what she did to him. She was the one who slept with Alan – his BEST FRIEND – during the weekend when Dad went away to have a break from all their arguing. She was the one who took Dad back and kept quiet when she realized she was pregnant. And she was the one who would probably have taken her secret to the grave if Alan hadn't told her that he loved her and wanted to be with her, when I was ten.

If she'd been a good person, she'd have told Alan where to go. But she didn't – she decided to tell Dad everything … even that I might not be his child. That's why Dad left and went to live with Granny Bennet. And THAT'S why Grandma Robinson hated Alan so much. There I was thinking she was jealous about not being in control, when she had it right all along – Alan had poisoned the mind of her daughter. Mediator my ass!

I'd have a little more respect for Alan if he'd run off to Australia and STAYED there when Mum took Dad back. But no. Alan only left after making them sign a letter granting him a DNA test when I was eighteen. Imagine the pressure Dad must have been under – the bloody ticking bomb in his head – yet he still brought me up as his own, never once treating me differently. Never. EVER. Not even when I used to parade Alan's half-birthday and birthday cards.

After it all came out back in July, it didn't take long for me to work out that Dad hadn't turned clean-up mad and accidentally thrown away my last half-birthday card. He'd had enough and snapped. So the one good thing to come out of this mess is the DNA test proving that I'm NOT Alan's child but one half of Reg Archibald Bennet. ☺

3.30 P.M.

Great news. I'm going to be an auntie! Malibu announced her surprise over lunch. She's three months pregnant. Dad looked chuffed to bits. "Have you told your mum?"

"No chance," Malibu replied.

"Too bloody right," I agreed, glad she was sticking to her guns.

"Now, girls," Dad said, and then he gave us his lecture about needing to forgive her. "Because, believe me, I wasn't perfect," he told us.

I was about to reply, "Yes, you bloody well were," when Robbie phoned and interrupted. He couldn't find a top he thought I'd washed – and when he realized I hadn't put the washing in the machine yet, he started to have a go at me.

"I don't ask for much. I mean, what the hell do you do with your time?" he asked.

Instantly I knew he mustn't have been picked for the

game tomorrow (he's always in a right mood when that happens), so I told him I'd hurry home.

I got back about half an hour ago and he's still sulking. He's on the phone to his agent now, saying that he hates his manager. Personally I don't think it's that bad. He hasn't been completely dropped for the game – he's a substitute.

Oh well, I'll be treading on eggshells for the rest of the night!

To cheer him up, I'll try that shepherd's pie recipe that his Mum dropped round yesterday.

Saturday 18 October – 9.30 a.m.

I pretended I was asleep while Robbie was on the phone to his mum, telling her my shepherd's pie wasn't half as good as hers. And I don't know why – I've never even wanted to be a good cook – but a hot tear dropped out of the corner of my eye and rolled down my cheek.

I couldn't bear to hear any more, so I tossed and turned to make him think I was waking up.

"Anyway, Mum, don't worry, I'm just gonna show what I'm about when I get on the pitch," he said, changing the subject.

She said something back and then he told her, "All right. See you for Sunday lunch, yeah?"

Oh no, not again, I thought. Not another chance for her to show off her perfect Sunday roast with the roast potatoes cooked just how Robbie likes them – in goose fat, crispy on top. So bloody what! The way she panders to him you'd think Robbie was her only child, but he isn't – he has two lovely but seriously neglected sisters. And I don't want to sound like I hate his mum, because I don't, she's actually a nice woman. But she has a big problem – she thinks the sun shines out of her son's ass.

1 P.M.

Robbie's dressed. I've still got the hump with him, and he's still being a miserable git, but I have to admit that he looks absolutely top-drawer today. He's wearing a black suit with a pink shirt and tie.

I've decided to wear the D&G polka-dot dress he bought me. You have to make a real effort when you go to watch home games because all the wives and girlfriends check you out – and they snigger behind your back if they think you're wearing something cheap. It doesn't matter what it looks like as long as it's bloody expensive. This dress cost £800! Robbie got it for me to wear to the second home game of the season (he hated what I wore to the first one), and when he picked it out and I looked at the price I literally started to shake. I couldn't believe it. But I'm used to it now.

"For fuck sake," he's just called up the stairs, "we ain't got for ever, you know."

I remember when he wouldn't swear in front of me –

that changed bloody quickly. (Except for the "c" word – he won't say that when I'm around.)

I'd better go.

6.30 P.M.

Yay! Robbie scored!! Netherfield Park Rangers: 1, Everton: 0. Thank God. He looked miserable sitting on that bench during the match. Probably as miserable as I felt sitting there watching – I still don't understand the first thing about football, so watching a game is even more boring if your boyfriend isn't actually playing.

Will Travis, who is to Robbie what Kellie USED to be to me, was the one who nudged me when Ivan Oyenko, one of the Netherfield strikers, got injured. I looked over at the substitute's bench and, sure enough, the manager was telling Robbie to get out of his tracky bottoms – he was substituting Robbie for Ivan with twenty minutes to go. My stomach churned because I knew how much Robbie wanted to score.

Will kept jumping up out of his seat and shouting, "Different class, mate! Different class!" whenever Robbie did something well. "It's confidence, Rem," he explained to me every time he sat back down. "That's all he needs."

When Robbie made a run back and tackled an Everton player, I thought it was a mistake because he's supposed to score goals, but Will clapped and said, "He hasn't changed a bit since the Rockingham Wanderers days."

I took a deep breath, expecting Will to harp on about their time playing together (from the age of six to eleven in the same Essex Sunday League team, etc., etc.) but he spared me. Or should I say Darren Hargreaves (the Netherfield Park Rangers goalie) did, when he dropped the ball and it almost landed over the line.

Will clapped his hands to his head. "What a muppet!" he yelled. And Darren's wife Anna, who had been quite nice to me up until then and happened to be sitting two rows in front, turned around and gave me the filthiest look ever.

Seriously, I would rather have watched paint dry than seen an extra four minutes of the match, so I groaned when the extra-time board flashed up. It was still nil–nil at that point – and it didn't look like it was going to change, either, until Robbie won a free kick. He decided to take it himself, and he struck it so hard that it whizzed past the Everton goalie and into the top of the net. Even I jumped to my feet that time. It was Robbie's first goal of the season and it felt like a cloud had been lifted from over both of our heads.

When we got into the car to drive home, Robbie leant over and pecked me on the cheek. Will, who was sitting in the back seat, went, "Oi, you soppy git." But Robbie told him I deserved it.

"I've been a right 'c' to live with lately," he said. "Haven't I, princess."

"Um… You haven't been that bad," I lied.

Robbie's gone to training and I'm bored. So when Terry's girlfriend Paris called to ask if I wanted to go shopping with her, I said yes straight away. Paris isn't as bad as I first thought. She's still crazy, I admit — and she's still majorly orange — but she's the only one of the team's wives and girlfriends who ever invites me shopping.

The rest of the girls prefer to shop alone. I reckon it's because they want to make sure they buy the very latest designer gear before anyone else does. Someone like me still gets a kick out of being able to afford the clothes in the first place, but they've moved way past that. They get a kick out of having things *first*. And the smart ones put their names down on waiting lists months before things actually come into the shops.

Paris either has a solid-gold heart or thinks I'm no competition, but I don't care. I'm just grateful that someone will hang out with me in this bloody foreign country of Essex, where everyone is style crazy and dressing down means wearing a full face of make-up, a French manicure and designer jeans or tracksuit — with REAL Ugg boots. A place where wearing Fuggs (fake Uggs), like I used to, will make people gawp as though you've just murdered someone.

I have three pairs of proper Ugg boots now — chocolate brown, tan and black woolly ones that button up at the side. Today I've decided to wear my tan ones with my grey

Franklin & Marshall tracksuit, and I'm going to set the whole outfit off (OMG, I sound like James now) with my blueberry Balenciaga bag.

I'd never heard of Balenciaga before Paris explained that the bag I'd bought from Camden Market, with the long stringy leather bits to open and close the zip, was actually a Balenciaga copy. I'd used it when I went to Robbie's first match and apparently she overheard some of the wives and girlfriends laughing about it in the Ladies, so I threw it in the bin and she took me to buy a real one for £800!

So even though Robbie isn't keen on me hanging out with her, Paris is OK in my book. Today we're going to Stylissimo, our local designer boutique.

5 P.M.

OMG. I've spent £2,000 today and all I bought was two dresses and a pair of shoes! Admittedly the most major pair of shoes on earth – red, patent, strappy – but still. And Paris spent even more than me!

She's only just left. When we were in Stylissimo, Terry called her to say he was coming back to ours with Robbie, so she brought me home.

When we arrived, the boys were sat on the floor playing on the Xbox, 200% focused on the big plasma screen in front of them.

Terry glanced across at the gazillion Stylissimo

shopping bags in Paris's hands and said, "Been spending my money again?"

"That's right." Paris grinned. "You don't want me walking around like a tramp now, do ya?"

Terry just shook his head and carried on playing. "Take that, you muppet!"

We left the boys to it and went to hang out in the kitchen, but I had to keep going backwards and forwards between the two rooms because of Robbie interrupting all the gossip Paris was filling me in on: "Princess, can you bring us some beers?" ... "They're not cold enough – put 'em in the freezer for a bit." ... "Can I have a cuppa instead? You want one, Tel?" ... "Are those beers ready now?" ... "I could murder some toast with jam – no, butter first, THEN jam... Cheers. Oh, and some crisps as well – salt and vinegar."

Anyway, once I'd caught up on all the gossip, Paris told me about her plan. The Netherfield Park Rangers boys are going down the West End this Saturday, and she's arranging for us wives and girlfriends to go out too. Only it won't be to Faces (our local night spot) like usual. No, she's going to make sure we "accidentally" bump into the boys by going to the West End too. Paris hates them having boys' nights out because she thinks some of the players get up to no good. I honestly don't think Robbie is one of them, but I must admit, it would be good to make sure – so I told her to count me in.

When Terry and Paris finally left, Robbie turned to me and said, "She'd better spend all the money she can."

"Why?"

"Because she's going to be binned any second now," he replied. "She's trouble, that girl. Don't waste your time hanging out with her."

Saturday 25 october – 11 a.m.

I know I don't write as much as I used to, but nothing that interesting happens to me any more. I wake up, shop, go to the gym every day (yes, the gym! I have to stay in shape), cook (well, attempt to) and go to Sak's once a week for a manicure and pedicure followed by Vidal Sassoon for a wash and blow-dry. That's about the long and short of my week. And when I read this diary back when I'm old and grey, I'm not going to want to hear about that stuff – I'll only want to know about the exciting things. The DRAMA. I reckon tonight might fall into that category, because the boys are off to the West End for the night and they have no idea that we wives and girlfriends will be there too!

1 p.m.

Decided not to give up on Kellie, so I gave her a call and invited her to our girls' night out. It wasn't easy, though. We've been best friends since primary school and Kellie has always been my confession stop. She knows about my first kiss, my first bra, the first time I had sex, and yet I felt nervous ringing her, like I needed to warm her up before I pounced with the question.

"Guess what? Malibu's preggers!" I announced as soon as she answered. It worked perfectly.

"What?!" she squealed. "No way!"

She wanted to know who, what, why, when. So I told her a bit and then baited her with, "Let's meet up later. We're having a girls' night out and I'll fill you in with the details then."

"OK. Where?"

"Dinner at a place called Sketches first, then hitting the clubs," I told her.

"Um, not sure about dinner… Might be a bit too early… Um…"

I realized she was probably backing out because she was short of cash so I said, "Dump the dinner, then, and just come for the clubbing. Paris has got us on to loads of guest lists."

"OK then," she finally agreed.

Yippee! ☺

<u>7.15 p.m.</u>

Robbie has just left for his night with the boys smelling like a bloody aftershave factory. He was also in the best mood ever. He had a Black Eyed Peas tune on repeat, which he sang along to at the top of his voice while he got ready, blatantly rubbing my nose in it about how good he was expecting tonight to be.

172

A part of me knows it was because the team beat Tottenham today and Robbie scored again – "a half-volley just on the edge of the box!" (WTF?)

But another part of me can't help thinking that Paris might have a point about some players misbehaving tonight. And although the other day I was confident that Robbie wouldn't be one of them, today I'm not so sure.

"Why aren't girls allowed to go too?" I asked Robbie earlier. "What have you lot got to hide?"

He made these big puppy-dog eyes and said, "Babe, don't have a go at me. I didn't make the rules." And it made me feel like I was being paranoid, so I left it. But when I saw him singing his heart out with the joy of bloody spring, I was glad he didn't bother to ask where we girls were going. And I'm glad that I'm actually going to be right on his big-headed backside!

He'd decided to wear his grey Armani trousers and powder-blue Ralph Lauren shirt, and he looked so–oo sexy but bloody well knew it. And it occurred to me that the girls in the club – or clubs – he'd be going to tonight would know it too.

It took me back to the time we first met in the Lounge, following Malibu's plan to snare ourselves a footballer, and I suddenly realized that tens of girls in the clubs tonight would be doing exactly the same thing. I wanted to say let's forget this boys'/girls' night out crap and just go somewhere together, but I didn't have the guts. So I decided to do the next best thing – make him feel just as insecure as I did.

I slipped into the leopard-print Vivienne Westwood dress I'd bought from Stylissimo the other day. Leah, the shop assistant, said it was the sexiest dress of the season. And she must have been right because Robbie's eyes nearly popped out of his head when I strutted up to him as he was about to leave and said, "What do you think?"

"Fuck me. Who are you trying to impress?"

"You don't want me walking around like a tramp now, do you?" I said cheekily, stealing Paris's line.

"No, course not," he mumbled.

And methinks I detected a twinge of insecurity. ☺

Sunday 26 October – 10 a.m.

This is about to be one epic entry, because last night was PURE DRAMA. Such a shame – it started perfectly. Paris had booked a limo. Not just any limo, but a big fat Hummer! I screamed when it turned into the drive.

"Paris, you're the best!" I said when I got in. She was sitting with her back to the driver, a champagne flute in one hand and a bottle of champagne in the other. Anna Hargreaves was beside her, and the rest of the girls all sat facing each other. The plush, pink seats had a purple trim, and the luminous tube lights that ran along the roof and floor of the limo flashed both colours.

Wicked. ☺

I took a seat next to Charlotte Murray, and then Paris leant over, handed me a glass and filled it with champagne.

"Now, girls," she said, raising her glass to the roof, "we're going to show them arseholes that we can have a bloody good time too."

"Yay!" we all cried like a bunch of St Trinian's school-girls. Then we lifted our glasses. "Cheers!"

In the car were Anna Hargreaves (the goalkeeper's wife – who seems to have forgiven me for Will calling her husband a muppet), Becky Robinson, Charlotte Murray, Claire Cunningham and, of course, Paris. I was the youngest there, followed by Becky (20), Claire (22), Charlotte (24) and Paris and Anna, who are both 25.

I've lived in London all my life, but in the past few months I've realized there are two Londons – one for people with money and another for those with diddly squat. Sketch, the restaurant we ate in, is for people with cash – tons and tons of it. The bill was £80 a head! Glad Kellie wasn't there – she'd have gone ballistic. The thing is, when she did join us it was clear she was determined to spoil the night. Yes, OK, the wives and girlfriends did talk about the carats of their diamond rings and name-check their designer clothes, shoes and handbags. And, no, we shouldn't have gone along with Paris's idea to go to every flash club in the West End until we "accidentally" bumped into the boys. But as I explained to Kellie, it wasn't the boys we didn't trust, it was those bloody WAG wannabes. And if she hadn't been so set on wrecking the night, maybe she would've understood that.

"This is pa-the-tic!" she said when we'd done a quick

five-minute search of our third nightclub – and left once we'd realized the boys weren't there.

"Shush, Kel!" I said. The limo had just drawn up to ferry us to another club and the rest of the girls were up ahead, congregated on the pavement and about to step in.

"No, I won't shut up. If they don't trust their husbands and boyfriends, they shouldn't bloody be with them! And I'm NOT getting in that ridiculous limo, either," she said, folding her arms like a spoilt three-year-old.

"Come on, Kel, you're making a scene. What's wrong with you?"

"What's wrong with ME? What's wrong with YOU, more like? I remember when you wanted to do something with your life."

"What's that supposed to mean?!"

"You've changed," she said.

"No, I haven't," I protested.

"You have. When's the last time you even thought about owning your own salon?"

"It's different now. There's no time for all that."

"Yeah? Well, it doesn't look like you – or any of your new friends – do jackshit to me," she replied. "Oh sorry, I take that back. Except for … SHOP!"

"That's out of order, Kel."

"I'm calling it like I see it," she said. "And they've talked about nothing but clothes all night."

"It's no different from what we used to do," I pointed out.

"Well, that's where you're wrong," she argued. "We used to talk about clothes that we wished we could afford – that's dreaming. They talk about the clothes they've already bought – that's just showing off."

"You know what?" I said. "Maybe Malibu's right and you *are* just jealous of me."

"Malibu? Don't get me started on that liar! One minute she's talking about holding out for eight weeks, the next she's three months pregnant by someone she's only known for three months."

"So?" I said, getting angry.

"So do the maths, Remy – she probably slept with Gary on the first night."

Before I could answer, Paris shouted for us to get into the limo.

"Come on, let's go," I said.

"What, so we can try to find your blokes? No, thanks. I've had enough of your crap – and your sister's." And she walked off.

In the limo I kept thinking about what she'd said, but then suddenly James called, screaming and crying. I couldn't make out much, except that he was on Greek Street in Soho and he'd been beaten up. That was really close to where we were.

"Stop the car!" I shrieked at the driver.

"Remy, what're you doing?" Paris asked.

"I've got to go."

"But you can't – it's raining!"

"I don't care," I said, then jumped out of the limo and ran through the streets in my leopard-print Vivien Westwood dress and killer heels until I found James sitting on the pavement, sobbing.

He looked a sight. Apart from the fact that he was soaked, his left eye was a mini red balloon and his face was covered in blood. I threw myself down beside him on the wet pavement and put my arms around him.

"What happened, babe?"

James tried to hold in his sobs as he explained that a group of boys had been shouting insults at him – poofter, fag, homo and the like. In the end he'd got so fed up that he'd turned round and sworn at them – and that's when they'd laid into him.

"Then, when I was crumpled on the floor," he went on, "they spat on me and walked off. And d'you know the worst bit?"

I shook my head.

"The worst bit is that no one bothered to help me. No one. They were all too concerned about getting out of the rain."

"Well, I'm here now," I assured him, and gave him a peck on the cheek that made him break into a smile.

We wondered what to tell his parents (they have no idea he's gay) and decided to say he'd been mugged. Then I hailed a cab and we both stumbled into it, soaked to the skin. When we got to his house, his dad was in bed but his mum heard us and came to the door. She was v.

shocked and emotional at the sight of her "darling James" and took charge straight away. They live in the nice part of Hammersmith that Dad says longs to be Chiswick, and his mum is majorly posh – which surprised me – and has straight, bobbed grey hair. We cleaned James up and put him to bed, and his mum insisted I stayed the night. (Claimed I looked wet enough to catch pneumonia.) So I texted Robbie to explain that I'd be home in the morning and ended up sitting on the end of James's bed all night, chatting about everything from Brangelina to the fact that Barack Obama, from certain angles, is actually quite hot. It was nice to have our old friendship back.

I got home at about 9 a.m. Robbie offered to pay for a cab – which would've cost £85 – but I took the Tube instead because I wanted to feel like normal, "before WAG" Remy again. *See*, I thought to myself, *this isn't too bad. I haven't changed*. (Although I must have looked a freak in my ruined posh frock and heels.)

Robbie picked me up from the station. He looked majorly hung over and claimed that the boys' night out wasn't all that. I'd taken pictures of James's injuries with my BlackBerry, but when I showed them to him he just glanced at them without a drop of sympathy. "Well, if he wants to be gay," he sneered, as if getting beaten up was James's fault.

"Sometimes you're an ignorant git," I snapped.

And I can honestly say that right now, at this very minute, I HATE Robbie Wilkins.

"It's done it again," I said to Robbie just now.

"What?" he asked.

"Your phone – ringing once and then stopping." It was the third time it had happened since I'd got home.

"It's probably Will messing about."

"OR it's whoever it was in the middle of the night on Friday and the day before that," I growled.

"Which was WILL," he replied. He didn't look nervous, I admit, and he was just as calm as he'd been when I'd commented on it earlier, but I still said, "D'you think I'm stupid?"

"Check my phone if you don't believe me," he said. Then, as I considered it, he walked up to me, kissed me on the lips and whispered, "But you have nothing to worry about, princess."

So I let it go.

Now I feel like he conned me. I don't know why – maybe because of all the stories of cheating incidents I heard from the girls last night in the limo. They were:

(1) Goalkeeper Darren Hargreaves: 3
Anna Hargreaves: 0

Cheated on her with: a lap dancer, a lap dancer, and … another lap dancer!

Final result: To get her to stay, Darren bought Anna a new Porsche the first time, a Cartier watch the second time and a brand new diamond wedding ring the third time. She calls it her compensation.

(2) Defender Tommy Roberts: 1, Becky Robinson: 0

Cheated on her with: her own bloody hairdresser!

Final result: One hairdresser is now minus a massive clump of hair extensions, Becky has a new, "even better" hair stylist, and Tommy whisked her away for a weekend break in Dubai. "It's been win-win, really," she told us.

(3) Midfielder Jason Murray: Infinity
Charlotte Murray: 0

Cheated on her with: there isn't enough paper or ink in the world to write down all the names.

Final result: Charlotte has given Jason the name of the divorce lawyer she'll use if he does it again. The lawyer happens to be well known for getting WAGs a huge chunk of their ex-husband's future earnings. And now, Charlotte says, Jason's so under the thumb that even if a girl walked by him naked, he wouldn't turn his head.

(4) Winger Martin Cunningham: 1
Claire Cunnigham: 0

Cheated on her with: a Page 3 model – and it made the *Daily Star*.

Final result: Claire has had a boob job (which he paid for) and claims that they're even closer. But she looked down-right miserable to me.

(5) Midfielder Terry Dawson: 4 (that Paris knows about), Paris Adams: 0

Cheated on her with: in Paris's words, "a bunch of no-good tarts".

Final result: Paris has forgiven him each time because "they bloody throw themselves at him. Besides," she added, "I'm not leaving this relationship until I have at least an engagement ring to show for it."

I let them know I'd finish with any boy who cheated on me, footballer or no footballer, but Anna scoffed and said she used to say the same thing.

Got to go now – Robbie's shouting for me.

6 P.M.

Yet another Sunday afternoon spent listening to Robbie's mum go on and on about the way he played football yesterday, last week, last month, last year and the bloody decade before that. It's good to be proud of your child, but she really takes the biscuit – and if it annoys me, I can't imagine how his poor sisters must feel. They never complain about it, but I suppose they have to play their cards right, seeing as Robbie has bought one of them a Volkswagen Golf and the other a Mini. And today he announced that he's going to pay for me to take driving lessons! I have a very generous boyfriend. ☺

Mum has just sent me a text. It says: *I love you and will always be here for you.* And it made me break down. I never thought I'd hear myself say this, but I miss her so much. And I don't believe that time is a healer, as people always say. The longer it's been, the more it's hurt.

Decided to be brave and give her a call.

I began to cry as soon as Mum answered the phone.

"Remy," she said, "if I could change anything, it would be not to have hurt you and Malibu. I love you both so much."

"But you did hurt us. You did," I replied through tears.

"I know," she admitted. "The only thing I can say is that Alan is the love of my life, and I sacrificed that to keep the family together. I even stood by and watched him go to Australia to get away from me. I TRIED, Remy. But this time, just this once, I wanted to do something that was right for me. I hope you can forgive me."

I cried some more and said that I'd try to. Then, for the first time in years, I told my mum that I love her.

Almost told her that Malibu was pregnant, too, but realized it would be much better coming from Malibu herself. I'm sure I can talk her into coming with me to meet Mum.

When the call ended I felt an overwhelming wave of relief pass through me.

Monday 27 october – 10 a.m.

I'm worried about Malibu. I keep replaying what Kellie said on Saturday night. I knew Malibu was breaking the Wag Charter when she first spent the night with Gary, but I never brought it up and I didn't care – I was just glad she was trying to get over Lance Wilson. But what really scares me is that I've checked the dates and it's 100% possible for Lance Wilson to be the dad!

Just hope I can keep my mouth shut when I see her today. We're meeting Mum for lunch.

11 a.m.

Just texted Kellie to invite her to our house this Saturday for Robbie's birthday/Halloween party. This is my way of saying let's forget about what happened on the girls' night out (I haven't actually spoken to her since).

5 p.m.

A very tearful afternoon. We had lunch in an Italian restaurant called Scalini's and Mum looked absolutely amazing. She'd lost weight, her hair was done and she was wearing make-up – but, most of all, she had a glow in her eyes that I'd never seen before. It said "I'm alive", and I realized that no matter how much I hate what Alan's done to Dad, I'm grateful to him for making Mum so happy. (Although I don't feel ready to meet up with him yet.)

Then, just when it seemed we were clean out of tears, Malibu announced that Gary has asked her to MARRY HIM! And Mum started to cry again.

What?! I thought as Mum sprang from the table and threw her arms around Malibu.

I know I should have been happy for her, but all the stuff about pregnancy dates was still whirring around in my brain.

I did my best to plaster a smile on my face as Malibu went through Gary's romantic, on-bended-knee proposal, possible wedding dates (before baby/after baby), dress designers (Vera Wang kept getting mentioned – apparently makes wedding dresses for Hollywood royalty) and possible venues (a castle versus a country estate), and before I knew it, it was time for Mum to go.

We agreed to meet up again next week.

"Look at my beautiful girls," Mum said when she got up to leave. "I'm so happy for both of you." She touched Malibu's stomach, then bent her head to talk to the tiny belly bulge. "And YOU," she whispered, "so lovely to meet you, too."

After Mum left there was an awkward moment when I didn't know what to say to Malibu. The obvious thing would have been "Congratulations", but I really felt like saying, "Stop right now and take a long hard look in the mirror." So I cracked a joke instead. "Can I have the old Mum back and return this one to Disneyland?"

Malibu giggled. Then… Another awkward moment.

So I finally said, "Congrats! Wow. That was a surprise."

"Yep," she replied. "Sprung that one on me, all right. But he said he's old-fashioned and thinks we should be married if we're having a baby."

"Great," I said – in a way that even I thought sounded false.

I looked at her cute little belly, then at her face, then at her belly again and finally opened my great big mouth.

"Malibu, I've been thinking," I said. "About the baby."

"What about it?" she asked.

"Well, just … the timing," I whispered.

"The timing? What you on about?" I could tell she was about to act as though everything was all right, but I'd made up my mind. So I looked her in the eye and said, "Malibu, are you one hundred per cent sure this baby is Gary's?"

She looked shocked for a moment, then angry. "Bloody hell, Remy, stay out of this."

"Because if it isn't…" I continued, determined. "If it isn't and it's Lance's … you're going to be found out as soon as the baby doesn't come out mixed-race."

"Yeah? Well, it might do."

"Might? MIGHT?" It was like she was living in cloud cuckoo land. "What are the odds?" I asked.

"The odds?" she repeated, still sounding defiant. "The odds are…" Then finally her wall came down and she looked like a helpless little girl. "Fify–fifty," she mumbled, with tears in her eyes.

"Malibu." I sighed, putting my hands to my head. "How can you take that chance?"

"Because I have no choice!" she hissed back at me. "Don't you get it, Remy? I'm not like you." She took a deep breath. "Why d'you think Mum always used to say *I* should marry a footballer and not you?"

"Because you're prettier than me," I answered straight away.

"Of course that wasn't why," Malibu replied. "It was because she knew you could go out and make something of yourself, but I can't."

That had never crossed my mind, but Malibu didn't look like she was trying to make me feel better about myself.

"Gary is my one and only chance of living like THIS," she said, holding up her finger with the huge diamond engagement ring on it. "And I'm not going to give it up."

6 P.M.

A bunch of Robbie's friends have come over – Will, Terry, Andy and Darren. They're having an Xbox tournament and then they're going to order a takeaway and watch some UFC DVDs. Robbie reluctantly told me I could watch them too if I liked, but I'd rather walk barefoot on glass.

Even though I've decided to stay in, I've put myself in the spare room that's furthest away from the living room, so I won't get distracted by their whoops or cheers – and I have my laptop with me. If Malibu, Mum, Kellie and Dad are all so sure I can make something of myself, I don't want to spend the rest of my life regretting that I didn't try. So I'm going to work on my old salon business plan.

Look out, Deborah Gordon – there's a new entrepreneur in town!

Saturday 1 November – 8 a.m.

Aa–aaargh! I've barely slept. So bloody tired. And pissed off. Three text messages beep-beeped for Robbie during the night – at eleven-thirty, one and then three. Each time I poked him and asked who it was and he mumbled, "I dunno. Probably Will." But there was another beep about fifteen minutes ago, so I decided I wasn't going to listen to his crap any more. I wanted to see for myself that he wasn't doing the dirty on me.

But now, of course, he's not so willing to have me check his phone. As soon as I ordered him to hand it over, he stormed out of the bedroom, saying that he wasn't going to be dictated to in his own house.

"Where do you think you're going?" I screeched as he yanked open the front door, having thrown on some jogging bottoms and a T-shirt.

"Off to clear my head!" he screamed back.

Or (in my opinion) to delete the incriminating text messages. ☹

<u>10 a.m.</u>

Robbie still isn't home. It's been two hours and his phone is switched off!

<u>10.30 a.m.</u>

Started to feel paranoid – it's Robbie's birthday party today and we've got loads of people coming. We need to do stuff to get ready for it, so I phoned Will to see if Robbie was with him. No luck there, so I tried Terry. Paris answered and told me that Robbie wasn't with them, either, so I explained what had happened.

"Do you think he's cheating on you?" she asked.

"I don't know," I said, honestly.

"Well, then leave him a message to say you're sorry and tell him to come home. It's his party today, why spoil things?"

"Hmm…" I could see her logic but didn't like hearing it. I suppose I wanted her to respond like they do on Jerry Springer – you know, "Kick him to the kerb, girlfriend! You got it goin' on all by yourself!"

But she didn't even come close. "Besides, he's treating you well, isn't he?" she said.

"Well-ish." I remembered (resentfully) how he'd had a go at me the other night for not using a coaster. My cup of tea left a round mark on the surface of his wooden coffee table and he acted like it was the end of the friggin' world.

Never did I imagine living with someone who's more of a cleaning freak than Mum, but he is. He straightens pictures, absolutely hates it if I drop a microscopic piece of chocolate in his car and even arranges our toothbrushes so that a perfect horizontal line can be drawn from mine, on the right of the sink, to his, on the left. He's nuts. (And I wish I could say, "He's nuts but he's the love of my life", but I'm starting to think that maybe he isn't.)

Obviously I couldn't say that to Paris, but I still tried to get the "You go, girl!" back-up I'd been looking for by telling her I plan to start earning my own money by opening a beauty salon. Unfortunately, Paris was on a totally different planet. She couldn't understand why I'd want to work and said that wanting my own salon was even more reason to play my cards right with Robbie – he could easily pay for one. She sounded shocked when she realized I hadn't even considered that.

"I want this to be MY thing. Something that's totally separate from him," I tried to explain. "My independence, I suppose."

"Forget that," she said. "What's the point of independence without a pot to piss in?"

OMG. Just heard Robbie come back in! Not sure

whether to ignore him, still demand to see his phone or play my cards right like Paris suggested and apologize. Hmm.

11 a.m.

I didn't need to apologize because Robbie came upstairs to find me and say sorry! ☺

"I shouldn't have walked out like that," he said. "I just can't stand being accused of something I haven't done."

He made those puppy-dog eyes again, big and blue, and it's so hard to have the hump with him when he does that. Then he cupped my face in his hands and said, "Now, if it means that much to you, princess, you can see the phone – but there's nothing to worry about. You're one hundred per cent the girl for me."

And I thought, *You've deleted the evidence, haven't you, you little shit!*

But I decided that maybe Paris was right – maybe I could get a salon out of this. So I closed my eyes and let him kiss me.

7 p.m.

Yay! It's ended up being a great day. Robbie scored again, this time against Manchester City (final score: 1–1) and now we've got his birthday/Halloween party to look forward to.

We've hired a marquee that can hold a hundred people,

and it even has a parquet dance floor (v. expensive). The party planners have sprayed the ceilings and corners of the marquee with fake cobwebs. They've also dotted pumpkin lanterns around the garden, and with a full moon and a sky clear enough to see a few stars, it looks absolutely magical. ☺

I'm about to get into my witch's outfit with the specially raised hem that makes it sexy.

Robbie is going to wear a Dracula costume (if he ever gets out of the shower) and … OMG, just realized he's left his mobile phone on the bed! OK, I know I shouldn't look…

But I don't bloody care!

scan the code for extra content:

Tuesday 4 November – 9 a.m.

Message one on Robbie's mobile read: *Hey sexy boy when are we meeting up again?*

I scrolled down for his reply and found: *Im working on getting a pass princess. I cant wait to hook up with you again.* ☺ *xx*

PRINCESS?!

Message two said: *I love you so much xxx*

His reply said: *Luv U 2 xx*

WTF?!

The third message said: *When are you going to tell her?*

Then Robbie walked in from the shower.

I could have dropped the phone and pretended I hadn't seen a thing. Been like Paris, thought about getting that salon and turned a blind eye. And for a split second

I truly thought about it. But I couldn't do it. Because what really got to me wasn't that he was seeing someone else (even though that was gut-wrenching) or that he was calling her princess (even though that made it worse). What really took the piss was that he'd been so sure his puppy-dog eyes and gift of the gab would work on me that he hadn't even bothered to delete the bloody text messages. Robbie Wilkins thought I was a FOOL! And I saw red. My fists made a blur as they pounded into his chest.

I never want to see Robbie Wilkins again.

9.30 a.m.

Kellie's gone to school but her mum has just been in and brought me a nice cup of tea. Now she's given me some space and left me to chill out in Kellie's bedroom. Kellie has been brilliant. So much of what she'd said was right. I had changed – got completely caught up in WAG life. A lot of people would have loved the fact that I'd ended up with egg on my face, but Kellie didn't think twice about inviting me to come and stay at hers until I sorted myself out. She's a proper friend. The best in the world. But I know I can't stay here for ever.

I suppose I'll have to go back to Mum's and face up to her new life with Alan. ☹

11 a.m.

That bloody Nicole Walker just phoned. "Is it true you've split with your footballer?" she said. "I can't believe it. What you gonna do now? I knew he'd be a—"

Didn't hear any more because I ended the call.

Thursday 6 November – 10 a.m.

Been going over what happened with Robbie. He told me that he's known Chloe (the girl who was texting him) since he was eleven. She was his childhood sweetheart, who – and he kept repeating this – loved him when he was nothing, a no-mark with as much chance of becoming a footballer as anyone else. Which was why he couldn't just finish his little fling with her, even though I demanded it.

"How do I know you're with me for the right reasons?" he had the cheek to snipe, as if *I* was the one cheating. That's when my fists started to fly and I told him to stuff his party and walked.

I've been completely numb for four whole days now. When Robbie's birthday came on Monday, I thought the pain would be unbearable, but apart from checking my phone a few times to see if he'd sent me a message (no way was I going to send HIM one), I basically did and felt nothing.

Everyone's telling me it's because I'm in shock. Who knows? Whatever the reason, I haven't even managed to cry yet. All I do when I think about Robbie is feel burning anger inside. And it's not even him I'm most angry with – it's myself for being such a fool. Foolish enough to quit my job, foolish enough to almost, ALMOST, give up my dream to open a salon, and foolish enough to lose Spencer. And I know things weren't perfect with Spencer, but Malibu was right, I should have kept him as a fail-safe.

That's why I've decided to give him a call.

11 a.m.

In the past hour, I have finally dropped enough tears to flood London.

They started to flow as soon as I ended the call to Spencer, which gave me so much hope in the beginning when he answered my "I have something to tell you" with "I have something to tell you, too", but ended with heartbreak when I told him to go first and he admitted that he'd finally met someone who made him understand that I'd been right and we were better off as friends. ☹ Her name is Joanne and she goes to Loughborough University with him.

"She's amazing, Rem, you'd really like her," he told me.

"Oh, great," I replied, forcing myself to sound happy. (I'm not sure I did a good job.)

Anyway, my eyes filled up when he said he'd arrange for me to meet her when he came down at Christmas. Then we said goodbye and I threw myself onto the bed and cried and cried and cried.

Friday 7 November – 8.30 a.m.

Some offers just can't be refused. Take this one, for instance: live rent-free (till I start earning), have meals cooked for me and a bit of washing and ironing thrown in too. How fab is that? Yep – I'm moving back to Mum's. TODAY! OMG, living with her and Alan under the same roof – this is going to be interesting. I've decided to be polite to him but that's IT. No major conversations or laughs.

1 p.m.

My lovely big sis is driving over in the new BMW X5 that Goldenballs bought her as a having-a-baby present. It's full of my clothes and beauty products, which she kindly picked up from Robbie's house. I couldn't bear to face him so soon. On second thoughts, I can't bear to face him ever! I keep remembering all the sweet talk he used to give me – those little lines that always made me smile and now just make me want to reach for the nearest bucket. Ugh!

Malibu called as soon as she drove away from our – no, HIS – house and said that Robbie had asked how I was doing. "He looked proper gutted, Rem. I think he misses you."

"Yeah? Well, GOOD!" came out of my mouth from deepest, darkest bitchville.

3 P.M.

OK, so I'm home. And after a big hug for Mum and a polite hello to Alan, I rushed to set up in my old bedroom and found that it'd been painted bright yellow with white polka dots. ☹

Some things never change.

Saturday 8 November – 4 P.M.

Met Dad for lunch and once we got the tricky stuff out of the way ("Well … how is Alan being with you?", "Um… Actually, not too bad. But I hardly talk to him, to tell you the truth.") we got down to business.

Dad absolutely loves my salon business plan: three treatments (tanning, waxing, nails), the Tanarama booth and even its name – Ta-dah! Then I took a deep breath and made my proposal.

"So," I said, "how would you and Uncle Pete like to invest in the business?"

I told him how I thought it would work. For a 25% share, Dad and Uncle Pete would buy the Tanarama booth and the equipment. I'd rent out nail tables and equipment to three beauticians, which would cover most of the salon's rent, and the beauticians could keep what they made for themselves.

He looked over my three-year forecast, which shows me making profit at the end of the second year. "The

Tanarama booth alone has the potential to make fifty thousand a year," I told him, "and I'll also sell nail and beauty products."

"How much do you need?" he asked.

"About thirty thousand."

Dad looked thoughtful.

"But I plan to pay you back the full thirty thousand pounds within three years, plus let's say … five per cent interest on top," I told him. "And if I do, the salon becomes one hundred per cent mine."

Dad raised his eyebrows. "You drive a hard bargain."

"It's business, Dad," I said. "Don't take it personal."

And he laughed because that's the title of Deborah Gordon's autobiography.

"Well, in that case," he said, once he'd finished chuckling, "as long as you agree that we can always retain a ten per cent share, I'm sure I can convince your Uncle Pete."

"Deal," I told him. And then we shook hands. Yippee!

7 p.m.

OMG. Kellie just called and said out of the blue, "We're going to Turkey!"

"We ARE?" I replied, shocked.

"Yep. A couple of weeks before your birthday."

"But I can't afford to, Kel, I'm putting everything I have into my salon."

"Shut up," she said. "I know that – that's why it's on me."

"No–o! I can't let you spend that kind of money!"

"It's gonna cost peanuts, trust me. A little, ahem, deal I've just negotiated."

I sighed. "Who is he, Kel?"

Then her voice completely changed. "OK, then, Mum, see you later." Then she whispered down the line, "I'm with him right now", and she was gone.

Yay! I'm going to Turkey! ☺

Sunday 9 November – 11 a.m.

So Kellie happens to have met the only straight male flight attendant on the planet. OK, so I've only flown three times (to Majorca, Majorca and Majorca) but I've seen nearly every episode of *London Airport* and all the male flight attendants on that show are as camp as a row of tents. But not this one. His name is Jack (after his English mum's favourite uncle) Ozdemir (he has a Turkish father), and according to Kellie, they've been head over heels for two whole days now.

Two days?! Well, it must be for real. LOL!

I hope that doesn't sound too bitchy. I'm happy for her, but I also happen to know what Kellie's like. If I'm honest, I'm just hoping she doesn't fall out with him by December because he's arranged our seventy-five-pounds-each-flight-plus-accommodation trip to Bodrum in Turkey, and I can't wait!

Monday 10 November – 9 p.m.

Met Dad and Uncle Pete for a talk.

"Have you identified premises yet?" asked Uncle Pete. "Have you decided what area your salon is going to be in? And whether you'll have any competition? These are the things I need to know." ☹

Come back, Kara, all is forgiven.

Tuesday 11 November – 1 p.m.

I've managed to find a few interesting salon options on-line: two are local, three are in Shepherd's Bush. I've called up the landlords and made appointments to see them this week.

Friday 14 November – 5 p.m.

If I see one more expensive-for-no-good-reason premises, I'll scream! Landlords want to charge a fortune for just a building with four walls and a lick of paint! Grrrr.

6 p.m.

I'm meeting James for a drink and catch-up this evening, and I'm so–oo looking forward to it. He always cheers me up. (Mainly, I admit, because he makes out that I'm so bloody wonderful.)

Something strange happened tonight. James was complaining about the boss of the hair salon he works in, but all of his gripes about what his boss expects him to do seemed like reasonable requests to me. Realized I'm on the other side now and that's probably how my beauticians will be complaining about me.

But the biggest surprise is, I'm starting to think that maybe – just MAYBE – Kara wasn't so bad after all.

Does that make me a mentalist?

Monday 17 November – 9.30 a.m.

And the Great Salon Hunt goes on. Aa–aaaaaaaargh!

Friday 21 November – 3 p.m.

Yay! I've just seen the best building! It has one large room with enough floor space for nail bars and a (v. grotty but easily replaced) sink at the back, plus space for cupboards and a washer/dryer (for towels). There's also a smaller room at the back that's a perfect size for the Tanarama booth, and another room upstairs that can be used for waxing. And it's in a great location – only twenty doors down from Kara's. ☺

Monday 24 November – 7 P.M.

"I like it," said Dad.

"Not bad," added Uncle Pete, nodding. (Uncle Pete is like the Simon Cowell of our partnership – we always want his approval.) "But what about the other salon down the road, won't it be hard to get customers?"

"Kara's?" I replied. "I used to work there, remember? Her clients are a lot older than we're aiming for. They want skin lasering and stuff and are willing to pay a fortune. Our market is young women who want to be brown and manicured for a night out at a decent price."

Uncle Pete nodded again. OK," he finally agreed. "NOW I'm willing to go to the bank manager and ask for a loan."

Yay!!!! ☺

Tuesday 25 November – 9.30 a.m.

Dad and Uncle Pete have a meeting booked at the bank! The only problem is that it's on Monday.

"Oh no–ooo," I said to Dad. "That's the day I'm going to Turkey. I'll have to cancel."

"Cancel? What for?" he replied. "You've done all you can do now. And if you ask me, I think you should take a break. It's going to be non-stop for you if we get this loan."

Wednesday 26 November – 11 a.m.

I know it's a bit sad but I've already started to pack for my trip to Turkey!

Dear God, please don't let Kellie fall out with Jack before Monday. ☺

Monday 1 December – 2 p.m. Turkish time (that's midday to those who are freezing their asses off in London, tee-hee!)

Jog on, miserable grey. Hello–ooo Bodrum, Turkey – clear blue sky around one huge spot of glorious yellow. Now we're talking!!

Jack (dark, good-looking and wears his furry eyebrows very well) is spending the holiday with us and he's taking us to the port this evening. He says there's a great English bar there called Lenny's. Bring it on. ☺

Midnight

Boys are the last thing on my mind, and that's probably why I met a gorgeous one tonight. ☺

The port of Bodrum surprised me. I've never thought of Turkey as rich or glamorous, but it's well classy – there are some incredible yachts in the harbour. Earlier this evening I spent ages staring at them, wondering what on earth these people did for a living to be able to afford them.

And for a brief second I thought, *If I'd stayed with Robbie, I could have lived like that.* But it was only very brief – and probably brought on by the fact that they were showing a Premier League Monday-night football match on the big screen in Lenny's. Yuck! I'd spent months having to watch bloody football and I wasn't about to watch another match tonight, not now I had the choice, so I went for a walk around the harbour and that's when I met this boy. His name is Stephen Campbell. He's Scottish, with a mop of thick brown hair and lips that were made for kissing, and he's on crutches because he's had an operation on his knee.

He caught me off guard. I was leaning on a barrier, staring longingly at one of the yachts in the port and I'd literally zoned everybody out – all the couples and groups of friends drinking and chatting outside the various bars – until I heard a voice behind me say, "How the other half live, eh?"

And I turned around to see Stephen's gorgeous face smiling at me.

"Yeah." I sighed dreamily. "They're amazing."

Instead of walking on, he stood there shyly, not saying anything. I could feel myself starting to blush because I thought he was a bit of all right, so to cover it up I pointed at his crutches and asked how he'd ended up like Long John Silver.

He gave a chuckle. "No, I haven't got one leg just yet, merely a very suspect knee."

"What happened?" I asked.

"A wee ligament problem, but I've had an operation – it'll be fine." He dismissed it as if it was nothing. I couldn't help smiling at his lovely accent and the way he'd used the word "wee". "It was written by a Scotsman, you know," he added.

"What was?"

And when he said *"Treasure Island"*, I thought, *Wow, a man who actually reads.* (Robbie wouldn't know *Treasure Island* if it fell from the sky and hit him on the head.)

Then a massive roar went up from Lenny's, so I guessed someone had scored.

"Not watching the football?" I asked him.

"Och, no! I get enough of that at home. What about you?"

"Me? I'd rather stick a hot needle in my eye."

He laughed. "You can't hate it that much!"

I thought of Robbie. "Oh yes I can."

He raised his eyebrows. "Well, that's refreshing to hear, because all the pretty girls I meet in Glasgow seem to be obsessed with football." Then he added, "Well, footballers, anyway."

"Poor fools," I couldn't help saying.

"I agree with you," he replied. "But then again, I would."

I smiled. He smiled. And then he gazed at me without saying a word. I've never in my entire life wanted a boy to ask me out more than I did then. So I decided to take a leaf out of Kellie's book (a much more subtle one) and went for it.

"How long are you here for?" I asked.

"Two weeks," he replied. "You?"

"Snap," I said.

We worked out that he was leaving one day before me. Then I asked who he'd come with and he told me he was on his own – a friend of a friend had got him a deal on a plush hotel so he could recuperate. When he asked me the same thing, I told him I'd come with my best friend and her man.

"They're proper loved-up. I feel a bit of a lemon actually," I said.

"Where's your boyfriend then?" he asked.

"I don't have one." I couldn't have told him quick enough. He looked pleasantly surprised.

"Well … maybe we should meet up," he said. "Go see the ruins or something. If you're up for it, of course?"

And I thought, *Of course I bloody well am!* ☺

Sunday 14 December – 10 a.m.

I can't believe that in an hour I'm going to have to say good-bye to the best guy I've ever, ever, ever met. And I don't know whether to tell him that us lying on his hotel bed last night and him telling me we shouldn't go any further until we're back home in the real world, then holding me in his arms until the sun came up, was most definitely number one in the top-ten moments of my life. How do I tell him that?

Or that five of those top-ten moments have been in these past two weeks: visiting the ruins at Halicarnassus with him (one of the seven wonders of the world), our first kiss on the beach (when I realized those luscious lips weren't just for show), when he told me he may be only twenty-two but he's met a lot of girls and I'm the only one he wants to be with twenty-four hours a day, and the moment when he said he might be moving to London in the new year and would love us to continue seeing each other.

"If you're up for it, of course," he added in his shy way.

This time I knew him well enough to say, "Too bloody right I am!"

I love so many things about Stephen, but one of the best things about him is that he doesn't look bored (like Robbie used to) whenever I speak about the salon. In fact I think he actually likes the idea. And I know it sounds corny, but I really believe that Stephen was sent to me by the universe, because he's made me realize that Spencer and Robbie and everyone else I've ever gone out with – or had a crush on (even YOU, if you're reading this, Mr Leonardo DiCaprio) – weren't right for me. Stephen Campbell is most definitely THE ONE. ☺

11.30 a.m.

I couldn't help it. When Stephen came to the hotel to say goodbye, I burst into tears.

He hugged me, and as he squeezed me tight, he whispered in my ear, "Don't cry, gorgeous, we'll be together in a few weeks."

"I'm going to miss you so much."

"I'm going to miss you, too," he said. And when he kissed me it felt like the ground fell away and I was floating on air.

Monday 15 December – 9 P.M.

Well, I'm back. Knackered. And the first person I texted when I landed was Stephen.

Me: *I'm home baby.*

Stephen: *Welcome back but you should be here, in Glasgow. With me. x*

10 P.M.

I phoned Malibu and told her all about Stephen.

"What does he do?" she asked.

"He's between jobs at the moment," I replied. "But he does a bit of this and that."

"This and that? What the hell does that mean?"

"I dunno, sells cars sometimes and computers, and … he didn't really go into it," I admitted. "But he's not a criminal or anything."

"You HOPE," she said.

"No. I… I just KNOW," I replied.

I've been summoned to a meeting with Dad and Uncle Pete. And Dad didn't sound too happy over the phone. Maybe the bank won't give them the loan. ☹

1 p.m.

Dad began the meeting.

"Which do you want first? The good news or the bad?"

I started to get scared. I'd always known they might not get the loan, but now I suddenly realized I had no idea what else I could do with my life. I'd set my heart on the salon.

"Have you heard from the bank?" I asked.

"Yes," he replied.

I took a deep breath. "In that case … the bad news first."

"Well," he began in a serious tone, "the best way to put it is that the next six weeks are going to be really tough for you – but I'm sure you'll start moving forwards after that."

"I'm sure you will," agreed Uncle Pete.

"Oh," I groaned as all the life was sucked out of me, "you didn't get the loan."

"No," said Dad. "We DID!" Then he opened his arms and threw them around me, laughing, as Uncle Pete stood in the background and beamed.

"Dad! You are so–ooo going to burn for that!" I told him

with the biggest grin ever known to man.

I can't believe I'm actually saying this, but *I am going to open a salon in six weeks! Ama–aaaaaaaaazing!!!*

Thursday 18 December – 8.30 a.m.

Happy birthday to me! Happy birthday to me! I am now eightee–een. Happy birthday to me!

Today I'm going to buy paint for the salon now that I've employed a painter/decorator and decided on the colour scheme (matt white with a deep-pink back wall, just like in my dream). ☺

Tonight I'm going out with Kellie, Jack and James, but I'm going to take it easy and only have a couple of drinks because I have so much work to do.

Can't believe that just when I can finally legally go out on the lash, I have to be a sensible businesswoman who's on top of her game. (Interviewing potential beauticians tomorrow!)

9 a.m.

Just been delivered a beautiful bunch of red roses. Fifty of them! They're from Stephen, and in Mum's opinion they must have cost him a bomb. I sent him a text: *Thanks for the flowers. I love you sooo much!*

And he sent back: *You deserve it. And I love you too. X*
☺

OMG. I've just had a call from Robbie!

In my head I'd gone through this moment a thousand times. I'd see his name flashing up on my phone, laugh like a cartoon villain – Remy de Vil, hah! – then thrust my hand down on the end call button with all my might.

In real life I had a bit of a panic. But wanting to hear what he had to say got the better of me, so I answered it but with a bit of attitude. "Yeah?"

"Happy birthday, princess," he said. And I admit, hearing his voice made me soften a little (well, on top of him actually remembering my birthday).

"Thanks," I replied.

Then there was a lo–oooong pause when I didn't know what to say. Then Robbie eventually spoke again.

"I want you back, princess," he told me. "And I'm willing to do what it takes. I'll dump Chloe. OK?"

That was another moment I'd played in my head – the one where he comes back on his hands and knees begging for another chance and I tell him to go take a running jump. But again, in real life it didn't feel that simple.

"Um… I don't know what to say," I replied as a feeling of love began to surge through me – only it wasn't love for Robbie, it was love for Stephen. And if I ever needed proof that I wanted to be with Stephen, I suppose this was it. I knew exactly what girls like Malibu and Paris would say – get back with Robbie and live like a real princess, never having to worry about money again. Yet here I was about to reject a big-earning footballer for a man who's between jobs … but who just happens to be the man I love. Maybe it was stupid and maybe I'm going to regret it, but I said, "It's nice that you called, Robbie, but I've met someone else."

Robbie had the cheek to snap back, "Well, it's your fuckin' loss."

What a tosser!

Wednesday 24 December – 10 a.m.

Christmas Day tomorrow. It's not usually my favourite time of year (turkey – yuck!, Brussels sprouts – even yuckier, and don't even mention bloody mince pies!). But this year is different because I'll finally get a break from work on the salon. Been doing twelve hours a day flat out! Plus, this morning Stephen texted to say his job opportunity has come off and he's definitely moving to London! He'll be here on New Year's Day and it's the best Christmas present ever. ☺

Thursday 25 December – 9 a.m.

Merry Chri–iiiiiiiistma–aaaaas!

Already sent a dancing Christmas tree text to all my phone contacts. And a loved-up one to Stephen. ☺

Christmas lunch is at Malibu and Gary's. Mum and Alan have only been there once before (when I was in Turkey) and

I can tell they feel like a massive bridge has been crossed now they've been invited for Christmas Day. It'll be weird spending Christmas with Alan instead of Dad. Wasn't sure if I should go at first, but when I called to check what Dad's plans were, he said not to worry about him because he was spending the day with a friend. Something about the way he said that made me ask, "A lady, by any chance?"

"Could be."

"Wow, Dad! Is she hot?" I teased. "I don't want an ugly stepmother."

"Yes." He chuckled. "She's very hot."

Legend.

10 P.M.

Wasn't sure how today would to turn out when I realized Grandma Robinson was coming too. Obviously couldn't leave her by herself (she's always spent Christmas Day with us since Grandad died), but still, it wasn't ideal. Gary's mum was doing the cooking (good thing – Malibu could burn a Pot Noodle!) and even though she's actually closer in age to Grandma Robinson than to Mum, age seems to be the only thing they have in common. Mrs Johnson is very Christian and gentle – never curses or swears – whereas Grandma Robinson is, and always has been, badass.

The first sign that things might not go smoothly came in the car on the way there.

"What d'ya reckon she's gonna cook then?" Grandma

214

Robinson asked, as though Mrs Johnson was from another planet.

"FOOD?" I suggested.

"Remy, don't be so rude to your grandmother."

"Well, honestly, Mum," I groaned, as if Grandma Robinson couldn't hear me. "She's from Jamaica, not Mars."

"So WHAT?" Grandma Robinson said (she's never needed anyone to stick up for her). "She's not English, is she? She might cook something spicy that won't agree with these blood pressure tablets I'm taking, and I thought I'd check. So get off your bleedin' high horse."

"All right, Gran, sorry," I said to shut her up.

She'd never been to the house before, and when we pulled up at the gates she looked v. impressed. "Bleedin' hell," she gasped. "Malibu's done well for herself."

"Yeah," I agreed.

Then she gave me a look that said, "Poor Remy, this could have been your life too."

"Can't be easy for you," she said, gently patting my knee.

"It is, actually," I growled.

Grrrrr.

The golden couple greeted us at the door, Gary dressed in a stylish suit, Malibu in a floaty designer dress. She looks lovely pregnant, all glowing, with the neatest baby bump on earth.

"On best behaviour, please, Gran," I heard her whisper.

"What the bloody hell do you take me for?" Grandma Robinson grumbled.

The table was already laid when we got there. Eight places – four for us and four for Malibu, Gary, Mrs Johnson and Gary's older sister, Rochelle. Rochelle is thirty-five (way older than Gary) and was exactly as Malibu described her – a cinnamon colour, slim and quite pretty on the rare occasion she decides to smile. So different from Mrs Johnson, who has chocolate-brown skin and isn't really attractive at all, except ... well, except for the fact that she smiles almost all the time, which makes you warm to her and totally forget that she isn't that pretty.

Lunch was kicked off with Mrs Johnson announcing that she would bless the table. We all had to put our hands together and close our eyes. She spoke ve–ry slo–wly, probably thinking we wouldn't understand her otherwise, and it made me smile the way she said "heverybody". The worst part was that it went on for way too long and she took loads of pauses, which made me think that she'd finally finished, only to (disappointingly) hear her start up again. But I hid my disappointment – unlike Grandma Robinson, who sighed every time. By the time Mrs Johnson finally said Amen, and Grandma Robinson opened her eyes, Malibu was staring daggers at her.

Christmas lunch was huge, tasty and traditional – turkey, chicken and lamb with tons of veg (including yucky sprouts), rice and potatoes – and the compliments flowed.

"Can't tell you how good it feels to have a proper Christmas meal after years of barbies on the beach," said Alan.

"You must tell me how you made your gravy," said Mum.

"Yes, lovely," agreed Grandma Robinson. "And not at all spicy."

Like me, Mum and Alan held their breath, and I'm sure I saw a slight roll of Rochelle's eyes, but Mrs Johnson just chuckled and told her, "Yes, well, I didn't think your h'English stomachs could take my pepper." And that was it – ice, well and truly smashed to bits.

Gran and Mrs Johnson bonded even more when they discovered, over mince pies, that their husbands had died in the same year. They swapped stories, including some that I'd never even heard about Grandad, and Gran was so happy and chatty that it made me think maybe she wasn't such a battleaxe after all.

The evening ended up with a few games – Weakest Link, Deal or No Deal and Charades. Team Golden seemed to win all of them, and whenever Gary touched Malibu's belly she didn't show a scrap of guilt. In fact – and it might have been the winning, or because it was Christmas – sometimes Malibu actually looked in love with Gary.

With the games over and the Quality Streets and Roses decimated (I managed to nick most of the mini Dairy Milks, tee-hee!), it was time to leave. And to top things off, on the way home it started to snow.

A white Christmas. Can't get much better than that! ☺

Friday 26 December — 10 a.m.

Would normally hit the sales today, but of course every penny I have has been put into the salon. ☹

Saturday 27 December — 11 a.m.

Yay! Bill, the painter and decorator, is just like me. When I called him and moaned, "If I see one more James Bond movie..." he said, "Here, here!"

Anyway, he's agreed to come down to the salon and continue work until New Year's Day. ☺

Wednesday 31 December — 8 a.m.

Tomorrow will be a new year and a brand-new start. In about four weeks' time I'll be opening my salon! And I'm so happy about Stephen coming to live in London too. He'll be here tomorrow! I can't wait to see him. To hold him. To snog him.

Finally my life is just how I want it to be. ☺

Thursday 1 January — 10 a.m.

Aa—aaaaaaaaaargh, my head! Had far too much to drink last night. Went out with Kellie/Jack (they're practically joined at the hip) and James, who at midnight announced that he was going to come out to his parents. Hmm...

Methinks they may find camels in the North Pole first.

Would love to stay in bed, but I have to spruce myself up for Stephen. Yay! Just the thought of seeing him makes my heart flutter.

11 a.m.

My baby just phoned to say that he has an introduction to his workplace at about midday, then he'll call me when it's over so we can meet up for lunch. I can't wait!!!

"I've missed you so much," I told him.

"Aye. Well, I've missed you more," he said.

2 p.m.

Stephen hasn't called yet. Maybe the introduction has lasted longer than he thought it would. I'll give him a ring.

2.05 p.m.

Just got his voicemail, so I left him a message: "Hello—oooo. Where are you, baby? Call me." Then I blew him a kiss down the line.

3 p.m.

Still no Stephen. This really isn't like him. I hope he's OK. I'll try him again.

3.05 P.M.

Voicemail.

This time I left: "Um, babe. Where are you?" ☹

4 P.M.

I've left message after message. And each time I check my phone to see if he's actually bothered to contact me, I get angrier and angrier.

A thousand thoughts are going through my head – mainly, *Maybe I was wrong about him.* But it's hard to accept that Stephen might not be for real, that believing that I'd met The One was a big mistake.

I'm calling him AGAIN.

4.15 P.M.

"Stephen, what's going on?" I demanded when he actually answered. "I've been waiting here for hours and—"

"Well, you can just get lost!" he replied in a voice I didn't even recognize.

"What?!"

"GO. GET. LOST. And I don't wanna hear from you again," he said, sounding furious.

"I–I don't understand."

"And *I* don't understand how I coulda fallen for your lies," he snapped. "You deceitful little—"

"Lies?" I cut in. "What you on about?" I was so confused by his words, by the hatred in his voice, that my head was spinning.

"What was it you said back in Bodrum?" he asked. Then he put on an English voice, MY voice, and said sarcastically, "Girls who like footballers? Poor fools." Then he became himself again. "What a piece o' crap that turned out to be."

Then I realized where he was heading. I hadn't told him about Robbie because I just couldn't find the right moment – and OK, I admit, I thought it might sound a bit hypocritical after what I'd said when we first met.

"Look, I know I should have told you," I said quickly, "but I knew you wouldn't like it and I—"

"Thought you'd get away with it," he finished.

"No. Well … in a way," I admitted. "I didn't think it was that important."

"Yeah, 'cos it's not IMPORTANT to know that I've been targeted," he sneered.

"Targeted?"

"Yeah. Any footballer will do for girls like you," he went on. "But what you didn't bank on was me joining Netherfield Park Rangers!"

I was stunned into silence.

"NETHERFIELD PARK?" I finally managed to say. Then panic set in. "Stephen, I swear I had no idea you were a footballer! You just said you were between jobs!"

"Well, that's not what Robbie Wilkins would have me believe," he replied. "Remember HIM?"

He was being cruel now. "Obviously I do," I said.

"Nice guy, actually," Stephen continued. "Offered to take me for a drink. 'Och, no,' I said, 'I gotta meet a girl.'" Then he became angry again. "Shoulda seen his face when I told him your name. Says you'd do anything to be a WAG."

"If that's what Robbie told you, he's a liar! OK, I'm not saying it's never crossed my mind, but with you it was completely different. I genuinely, GENUINELY fell for you." There was silence. "Stephen?"

But he was gone. ☹

5 P.M.

I've Googled him. Stephen Campbell – Glasgow Rangers player. He damaged a knee ligament in a game against Dundee United six weeks ago and had an operation, and people were wondering if the English teams interested in buying him would change their minds. Because of his injury and all the pressure and speculation, his manager gave him some time off.

That's obviously when I met him in Turkey.

Well, Stephen Campbell, you have truly broken my heart.

<u>Monday 2 February – Salon Opening Day!</u>
<u>8 a.m.</u>

It has been the toughest few weeks of my life. I've literally grieved for Stephen as if he's died. I've thought of him as soon as I open my eyes and felt an ache in the pit of my stomach that has sometimes lasted a whole day. Without the salon to throw myself into, I don't know what would have become of me. But I just knew I couldn't let it fail. I've had to oversee the decorating, buy equipment, find staff, and finally I've spent the last few days leafleting what feels like every street in west London to announce the opening event. (I didn't want to rely on my Facebook post.) Here's what the leaflet looks like:

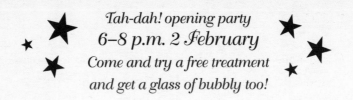

Tah-dah! opening party
6–8 p.m. 2 February
*Come and try a free treatment
and get a glass of bubbly too!*

The free treatment and drink was my idea. Uncle Pete (my very cautious business partner) didn't like it. He said that nothing in life should come for free. But I told him we needed a great promotion to get people through the doors in the winter months and then word would spread by spring. Then we'd have a great summer, which is the peak season for women getting treatments done.

I quoted Deborah Gordon at him (as I have now read her autobiography): "If you give something away, make sure it's something people will want again." And why wouldn't people want to pop into a salon and be golden brown within six minutes, with no damage to their skin?! Why wouldn't they want a great wax, and the hottest nail colours on earth from manicures and pedicures that are 10% cheaper than Kara's? My gamble is that they will, as long as the standard is good. And it will be – I'll bloody make sure of that. Dad (my more easy-going business partner) agreed with me. God bless democracy.

Today we have to buy the bubbly and snacks and make some last-minute touches to the salon to make sure it looks pristine. But most of all I want to enjoy tonight. This opening party feels like my reward, and I know it's going to be sheer hard slog after this.

5 P.M.

Came home to get ready and found the most fabulous Victoria Beckham dress on my bed! Opened the card lying on top of it, which just said: *Go get 'em sis! Love Malibu x*

I love Malibu so–ooooo much!

11 P.M.

I have a new number-one moment in the top-ten moments of my life!!

Tonight couldn't have gone better, even in my dreams. So many people turned up – friends, strangers, old work-mates (Natasha and Blow-dry Sarah) and even enemies! Tara (spit, spit) Reid couldn't resist the free champers, I suppose, but who cares? She set foot in MY salon and actually said something nice to me, for the first time ever ("Yeah, looks all right").

There were so many people that at one point we couldn't fit them all in and had to take snacks out to them on the street.

Mum came with Alan and tonight I was the nicest I've been to him for months. Mainly because Dad is clearly over Mum – a red-headed yummy mummy was on his arm when he arrived.

"Very nice to meet you," I said after Dad had introduced us.

"And you. I hear you're the new Deborah Gordon," she said, smiling.

Malibu and Gary were there, of course. Malibu's all protruding belly but is so skinny everywhere else, you can't even tell from behind that she's pregnant. Gary looked so happy. He kept touching her tummy, and seeing that made me hope even more that the baby is his.

Kellie/Jack came, still wrapped around each other at every given moment, and James was there too.

"How did it go with your mum and dad?" I asked, because I knew he'd chickened out of coming out to them three weeks on the trot, but he'd said yesterday was going to be the day.

"Um… Chickened out again," he confessed, and we both laughed.

Spencer arrived with his new girlfriend – who isn't too bad, actually. OK, I admit, she's great – bubbly and quirky, and definitely more right for him than me.

"I've heard so much about you," she told me.

"I swear it's all good," Spencer added.

Then … the Feminazi turned up!

"It will be very interesting to have some competition up the road," she said. "But I couldn't think of a better person to be up against." She smiled. "I knew you had it in you, Remy."

"Thanks, Kara," I gasped.

And it was in the middle of talking to her that I saw him standing just inside the door, smiling at me, still in possession of those bloody gorgeous lips.

Stephen? I thought. And I began to feel angry about all the unreturned calls. In my head I wanted to walk up to him, slap him in the face black-and-white-movie-style and say, "You cad!" But in my heart I couldn't help thinking, *Is that you? Is that REALLY you?*

I walked up to him, playing it cool, even stopping to say thanks for coming to a few guests. Then when I was finally standing in front of him, I tried to calm my heart – which was now pounding through my chest – by cracking a joke. "Hi, stranger. I almost didn't recognize you without the crutches."

"You did it, Remy," he said. "And I'm really proud of you."

He looked at me and my insides started tingling, and all the hurt formed a huge lump in my throat.

"You know," I began, trying not to cry, "you really should have given me a chance to explain."

"I've thought of nothing else for the last month," he replied. "And I'm hoping you'll forgive me, Remy, because I've missed you. I'd love us to try again… If you're up for it, of course."

And then Stephen Campbell put his mouth on mine and kissed me in front of the entire room.

NOW, I thought, *I know the meaning of perfect.* ☺

scan the code to read Remy's business plan:

Acknowledgements

With thanks to:
KT Forster
Helen McAleer
Gill Evans
Emma Lidbury
Annalie Grainger
Alice Burden and the rest of the PR team
Jo Humphreys-Davies and the marketing team
Kate Beal
Fiona MacDonald
Paul Rhodes
Sean Moss
Katie Everson
Jas Chana and everyone at GoSpoken
Mark Hodgson and Blackberry
Ruth Harrison and The Reading Agency
Caroline Odland
Tim Holloway

READ BETWEEN THE LINES

UNDERCOVER is the best
in young adult fiction from
Walker Books.

Scan this code to watch other
UNDERCOVER book trailers:

Get the mobile app
http://gettag.mobi

Turn the page to check out more
UNDERCOVER READS or visit
www.undercoverreads.com

**Lennie Walker – sisterless, lasagna maker,
Heathcliff-obsessed and hopelessly in love…**

*What kind of girl wants to kiss every boy at a funeral,
wants to maul a guy in a tree after making out with
her (dead) sister's boyfriend the previous night?
Speaking of which, what kind of girl makes
out with her sister's boyfriend at all?*

"The book of the year … this book is perfection."
Carly Bennett (blogger)

"Heart-warming."
Independent

"Entirely compelling."
Guardian

everybody has a secret

When Billie inherits her grandmother's house, it's a fairy tale come true. Maybe she can find the father she's never met. But moving back to her mum's childhood home dredges up secrets – and Billie soon discovers that people may die, but the past lives for ever.

"Billie Paradise is looking for a place to belong, and finds herself tangled up with the ghosts of the past... Beautifully written, emotionally powerful, a novel you won't forget."
Cathy Cassidy

SOME GIRLS ARE GLAMOROUS, BEAUTIFUL ...

AND DEADLY

If Callie Carson is found kneeling by the dead body of Katherine Remington-Day with a bloody knife in her hand, she must be the murderer – mustn't she...?

Joining the in-crowd is tough.
Leaving is a killer.

"We found him face down in the mud at Long Reach.
Near the Dartford bridge.
Looks like he might have jumped off."

EDDIE SAVAGE makes two shocking
discoveries in quick succession.

One: his brother, Steve, has been working undercover.
Two: Steve is dead.

Eddie refuses to believe that his hero elder brother killed himself,
and there's only one way to find out the truth: follow his footsteps.

There's a job: to infiltrate the notoriously violent Kelly family.
There's a girl: the boss's daughter — beautiful, sexy, dangerous.

Before long, Eddie is up to his neck in Kelly business … and sinking fast.

A gritty, glamorous thriller with a heart-stopping, brutal conclusion.